The Prince of Life

Robert T. Gamba

Order this book online at www.trafford.com
or email orders@trafford.com

Most Trafford titles are also available at major online book retailers.

Note for Librarians: A cataloguing record for this book is available from Library
and Archives Canada at www.collectionscanada.ca/amicus/index-e.html

Printed in Victoria, BC, Canada.

ISBN: 978-1-4120-1366-6

*Our mission is to efficiently provide the world's finest, most comprehensive book publishing
service, enabling every author to experience success. To find out how to publish your
book, your way, and have it available worldwide, visit us online at www.trafford.com*

Trafford rev. 08/14/09

North America & international
toll-free: 1 888 232 4444 (USA & Canada)
phone: 250 383 6864 ♦ fax: 812 355 4082

He Shall be Called

Isaiah 9:6
For unto us a Child is born, unto us a Son is given; and the
government will be upon His shoulder. And His name will
be called Wonderful, Counselor, Mighty God, Everlasting
Father, Prince of Peace.

The Prophet Isaiah receives a powerful revelation from God
about a Child, a Son that God gave to humanity by His
mercy. This is not just a Christmas message to be written
on a Hallmark card. It is the pure truth concerning eternal
life that waits for all those who are willing to receive it by
faith
Years before the birth of Jesus Christ in the flesh, God
reveals the most wonderful, exciting, joyful, inspiring news.
"A Son will be given," shouts the prophet with tears of joy. A
Son whose government will know no end. A Son, who will
redeem the lost, heals the broken hearted, give hope to the
hopeless, strength to the weak and life to the dead. A King
who rules an eternal kingdom built on the word of God. A
Prince of Peace who will fill the emptiness of all who receive
Him with a peace that surpasses all understanding. Every
ruler has a throne and every king has a kingdom, but this
Son's Kingdom will have no end.
His name shall be called wonderful, marvelous, and
magnificent. Wonderful, meaning also full of wonder,
amazement, to marvel, admiration, and supernatural power.
That is a good way to start describing this Child given to us
to heal our broken stained spirits. Jesus is known by many
names. He is called *the Lord, the Light, the Way, the Truth,*
the Life, the Good Shepherd, the Holy One, the Savior, the
Redeemer, the Sacrifice, the Anointed, the Apostle, the
Author of our faith, the True Vine, the Word, I AM, the Door,
the Christ, the First and the Last and the *Eternal King.* All
these names have attempted to describe the Son just as
many names are given to describe God the Father. The
Prophet Isaiah received a group of names in describing the
Lord of all lords. However, when we think of someone who

is beyond words, beyond description, the word wonderful comes to mind. Let us go back in time and think about someone who had given us something that we cherished, calling that person wonderful! Think of the first time that we realized that we had fallen in love. We describe that special person with the word wonderful. God places a very high value on names. A name in the Scriptures describes the very person's nature. God opens this revelation by calling His Son, wonderful! A word used when describing someone who is just so great that we have to settle for the word wonderful because of a lack of any other word known to man. Now that we know how wonderful this Child is, we can begin to explore all the reasons why.

The next name given to this person is *Counselor*. Have we ever given any thought of God being our Counselor, a counselor meaning someone to consult with? What a great insight this is from the heart of God. Which one of us would refuse to counsel our children? How much joy that would give us in knowing that our children respect our opinions in that they would come to us with a problem looking for direction. We have this wonderful option with God! He calls His Son a *Counselor*, someone to consult with, someone who will listen and direct us with wisdom and love. This can be accomplished through the avenue of prayer and His word. God offers free consultation, no fees, no contracts, or fine print. God wants us to be all that He has promised us to be, if we are willing to consult with Him. He is there, ready, willing and more than able to lead us in the direction of peace, joy and love. What a great revelation to know that God wants to be our *Counselor* as well as our Lord. For He is not untouched by our desires. He understands our struggles and hardships. His ear is open to our prayers.

Psalm 147:5
Great is our Lord, and mighty in power; His understanding is infinite.
Psalm 145:16

You open Your hand and satisfy the desire of every living thing.

A *Counselor* who knows all things, and who loves us and who understands what we feel in these fleshy shells. He is someone who can identify with all our sorrow and pain.

Psalm 145:19 and 20
He will fulfill the desire of those who fear Him; He also will hear their cry and save them. The Lord preserves all who love Him...

Have we ever really stopped and thought for one minute what God has done for us? I am not talking about all the blessings that He has given us with our children, jobs, and freedom to live in a land like America. I am not talking about our day-to-day blessing that He has gives us. I am talking about the gift that He gave of His very own being. He prepared a road that leads to an eternal home where sorrow, death, and tears no longer have any place. Where the brightness of His love fills every square foot of space, it is all waiting for us. It is ours, from the one who gave all He had to assure us a place where the joy of God lives forever. Jesus the Christ, *Wonderful* is His name. Let all of the heaven and every living thing sing to the Lord, blessing His holy name, *Mighty God, Everlasting Father, God with us!* Then we hear Him called the *Prince of Peace.* What does man desire after he has gained all the material wealth of the world, and has reached high positions in leadership? He builds towers and machines, cities and towns and makes laws to govern them. He discovers that none of these things would equal a moment of peace, the true peace of heart that comes from the *Prince of Peace* Himself. For all these other things we can pursue, but the greatest thing to capture is the very thing that God promises to give us free is peace! Here we read that there is a *Prince of Peace,* who is willing to impart His peace as we try in vain to learn it, buy it, capture it or obtain it. God promises to give it to us if we would only stop and listen to the counsel of His love. His peace is the harmonious relationship between the creation and the Creator. All of creation has this except for man. There is a peace, a contentment within nature that is in the silence of the living God. A strong but gentle presence that surrounds the earth, it is the peace of God. It is the very thing that our hearts desire; that our minds long to be touched with; it is right in our reach. This peace, the communion with God the Father through His Son Jesus Christ, is all and more of what our hearts could ever hope. It is a peace that is able to break through all our protective walls; all our barriers that have been built around us for protection from past hurts. When God's peace enters, the walls fall along with the fears and hurts that imprisons us. He is the *Prince of Peace.*

Micah 5:4, 5
He will stand and shepherd His flock in the strength of the Lord, in the majesty of the name of the Lord His God. They will live securely, for then His greatness will reach to the ends of the earth. He will be their peace.

John 14:27
Peace I leave with you, My peace I give to you; not as the world gives do I give to you.

God promises a peace that is not a matter of things around us being still and calm, but an inner peace that is not shaken by external circumstances, a peace that comes from the heart of Jesus Christ. His peace He gives to us, not the peace in that anyone else could attempt to copy; it is the peace of the living God. God tells us that He will make a covenant, a vow of peace between Him and His people.

Ezekiel 34:25
I will make a covenant of peace with them...

God promised the people of Israel that He would give them a peace, a blessing of security, so they may know that He is their God. That same peace is freely given to every person who is willing to come to the Son of God through faith. It is not through our self-righteous view of our image, but through pure faith, trusting God through His Son Jesus Christ, the *Prince of Peace.*

Hebrews 13:20 and 21
Now may the God of Peace who brought up our Lord Jesus from the dead, that great Shepherd of sheep, through the blood of everlasting covenant, make you complete in every good work to do His will...
Ephesians 2:14
For He Himself is our Peace...
John 16:33
These things I have spoken to you that in Me you may have peace. In the world you will have tribulation, but be of good cheer, I have overcome the world.

Is there a peace that can bring us through this unstable world? There is a peace that can bring us through the storms of life, even when the waves are crashing against our boats. Yes, there is a peace. How can we be so certain about this peace, God promised His peace to all that are willing to trust Him? However, we must come to Him by faith. There is a peace in Christ, a peace in knowing that all the mighty promises in the Scriptures are true and alive. There is a peace when all hell breaks out around us, yet God speaks to our hearts and says, *"Be still and fear not."* There is a peace in the security of knowing that God has given us His word to store in our hearts and minds and to use as a light that shines our paths. There is a peace that lives deep in our beings, that searches our hearts and breaths life into these bodies. There is peace in knowing that God spared not His Son, so that we may have the eternal gift of everlasting life. There is a peace in believing God.

Though the storm might be raging against us, there is His calm in us that is from the *Prince of Peace*, Jesus Christ. For He is our peace because in Him is all the fullness of life. *"Peace I leave with you, My peace"...* Jesus could not have said it any simpler than that. Peace that is in God is a product from having peace with God.

Romans 5:1
Therefore, having been justified by faith, we have peace with God through our Lord Jesus Christ...

Some might view these words as some kind of brainwashing that strips a person of their own identity. A robot factory that produces the same functions in a programmed tool designed not to think, but just do. This could not be any farther from the truth. Did you ever think about the fact that there is only one you? After all the millions, billions, and trillions of people who ever existed, there is no one like you. God does not want clones to look the same, talk the same and simply exist. God has made us unique yet unified. This is God's design; it did not happen by chance. To receive the peace of God, one need not be a robot, programmed to be a look-a-like, sound-a-like believer. On the contrary, God made us one cell at a time, different from anyone who ever existed and anyone who will ever exist again. God made us one at a time, and one of a kind. In knowing this we can have peace in Christ, for God loves us for who we are, but is looking to remove the very thing that wars against His peace, sin!

Proverbs 14:30
A heart at peace gives life to the body...
Philippians 4:7
And the peace of God, which surpasses all understanding, will guard your hearts and minds through Christ Jesus.

Jesus is the *Prince*, the Giver of God's peace. We will never receive the peace that He has reserved for us unless we make a real decision to trust Him with all our cares, with all our problems and with all our love. Jesus is our Lord, our King and our Prince who has given His all.

...Mighty God, Everlasting Father...

Jesus is revealed as *Mighty God* and *Everlasting Father*. I do not believe that this is a misprint or a case of an error in interruption. Rather, this gives us another insight into the nature of God. Jesus has been given all power, all authority and a name, which is above every name. Jesus was, and is, and will always be the living *Word of God*. He is the direct representative of every thought of God. After all, our own words are a representative of our thoughts. Even our most careless words began with a thought. In other words, Jesus is the manifest living action of God's thoughts. The prophet calls Jesus, *Mighty God*. Jesus is God presented in the natural, representing all that is holy. His peace and His rule will never end, but is from everlasting to everlasting. Unto Him, we believe with an eternal hope in a journey that is heaven bound, using faith as our transportation.

A Child was born; *Wonderful, Counselor*, who is called *Mighty God.*

Isaiah 9: 7

Of the increase of His government and peace, there will be no end...

My Son

Psalm 2:1
I will tell you the decree of the Lord: He said to me, "You are My Son, today I have begotten you".

Here we see a Scripture quoted by the Apostle Paul in the book of Acts, and again in the Epistle to the Hebrews, as some believe to be Paul. The quoted Psalm opens with man's attempt to run the planet as he sees fit, and to conspire against the Lord God, the Creator of all life. It explains that man has set his counsel against the Lord and His Anointed (Jesus), but the Lord laughs. Why is the Lord laughing?
Man's futile attempt to run the world according to his own greed will fail on its own. God knows this and continues to extend His hand for guidance. However, if man refuses, he will pay the consequences. God does tell us in this Psalm that one day He will set a King over all the earth, and His Kingdom will know no end. His Anointed, His Son, Christ Jesus will rule as Lord over the hearts of mankind. God tells His Son, *"You are My Son, today I have begotten you".* The question is when is, today? Is God insinuating that His Son was created on a particular day? Some teachings claim that Jesus was the first born of all creation and therefore deny His deity as God the Son.

Colossians 1:15
His is the image of the invisible God, the first born of all creation.

This Scripture does not stand-alone. Could Jesus be the first born or the first created being of all creation, before the foundation of the heavens and the earth?

Colossians 1:18
He (Jesus) *is the head of the body, the church: He is the beginning, the first born from the dead, that in everything He might be pre-eminent.*

The apostle is clearly stating that Jesus is the first born from the dead. This resurrected Man, different because this Man now has been glorified with an eternal body, being the first born from the dead of all creation.

Acts 13:32 & 33
And we bring you the good news that what God promised to the fathers, this He has fulfilled to us their children by raising Jesus; as also written in the second psalm, "Thou art My Son, today I have begotten thee".

The Apostle Paul received a true revelation that Jesus was begotten from the Father, who is the *first-born from the dead,* or we could say released from the power of death, thus fulfilling Psalm 2:1. Paul brings this Scripture as a point of reference that by the raising of Jesus Christ from the dead, on that day Jesus was the *first born of all creation* to receive resurrected eternal life as a Man. This has never been done before since there was simply no one who could supply such a perfect blood sacrifice for the full redemption of the sins of all men. Today, on the day that Jesus walked out of the tomb, He became a resurrected Son who was brought forth through the trial of death, by the power of His blood that was shed for us.

Acts 13: 34 & 35
And as for the fact that He raised Him from the dead, no more to return to corruption, He spoke in this way, 'I will give you the holy and sure blessing of David.' Therefore, He says in another psalm, 'Thou wilt not let thy Holy One see corruption.'

The apostle is no doubt writing about the power of the resurrection as he refers to the promises of God the Father, with all assurance that Jesus is the *first-born from the dead*, but will not be the only.
Paul had received a revelation of Mount Zion and the new city of Jerusalem as he explains his vision and the N new covenant of hope to us. This also reinforces that Jesus is the first born of many to come, from the dead.

Hebrews 12:22 & 24
But you have come to Mount Zion and to the city, the heavenly Jerusalem, and to innumerable company of angels in festal gathering, and to the assembly of the first born who are enrolled in heaven, and to the Judge who is God of all, and to Jesus, the Mediator of the new covenant...

The *assembly*, (all believers) *of the first born*, (Jesus Christ) who are enrolled in heaven are all those who come to the throne of grace by the blood of Christ, who have been cleansed by His blood and have been redeemed by faith in the power of the resurrection. Paul also tells us about an innumerable amount of angels, (too many angels to count) in a festal gathering, (a celebration) around the throne of God. Then there is Jesus, *the Mediator of the new covenant,* in all His glory, with every crown of honor on His head, Jesus, *the first born from the dead.* This is truly one of the greatest revelations of heaven!
Since the word is established by two or three witnesses, let us read what the Apostle John received in revelation by the power of God.

Revelation 1:4
Grace to you and peace from Him who is and who was and who is to come, from the seven spirits who are before the throne, and from Jesus Christ the faithful witness, the first born of the dead, and the Ruler of kings on earth.

The Apostle John's revelation confirms the revelation Paul received, that Jesus is the *first born of the dead.* Does God ever reference any one else as His firstborn? Yes!

Exodus 4:22 & 23
Then you shall say to Pharaoh, 'thus says the Lord: Israel is My son, My firstborn. So I say to you, let My son go that he may serve Me. But if you refuse to let him go, indeed I will kill your son, your firstborn"

God now uses the word *firstborn* in reference to the nation of Israel as His son, begotten of God. Does this insinuate that the nation of Israel was the *firstborn* of all creation? Israel was not brought forth as a nation until the covenant with Abraham was established between God and Abraham. Therefore, God uses the term *firstborn* to identify his covenant with Israel, signifying that Israel is like a chosen son. The word *firstborn* is symbolic to the relationship that God has with the nation Israel. This is one of those examples in that God references a word to describe His relationship with a nation or a person. It is obvious that when God is referring to His relationship, the word *firstborn* is symbolic and not referring to an actual first birth. So, does this hold true as we read in the Gospel of John in chapter three?

John 3:16
"For God so loved the world that He sent His only begotten Son, that whoever believes in Him should not perish but have eternal life".

The word begotten in this context is defined as one who has been fathered. Again, symbolic of a special relationship between the Son and the Father, not referencing a first birth experience. The Apostle John, through the Holy Spirit is revealing to us what kind of relationship they had witnessed.

John 1:1 & 2
In the beginning was the Word, and the Word was with God,
and the Word was God. And the Word became flesh and
dwelt among us, full of grace and truth; we beheld His glory
as of the only Son from the Father.

Once again, the apostle extends his testimony as a witness
to the deity of the Son of God as the only Son, which
expresses the special relationship in the Godhead between
Jesus and His Father; the bond of unity, devotion and love
toward one another. One purpose, one desire, one nature,
one God.
The writer of the Epistle to the Hebrews also uses *Psalm
2:1* as a point of reference to reveal the relationship
between God the Father and the Son of God.

Hebrews 1:5
For to what angel did God ever say, "Thou art my Son,
today I have begotten thee"?
Or again, "I will be to Him a Father, and He shall be to Me a
Son".

The writer, by the directive of the Holy Spirit again zeros in
on the relationship within the Godhead. The love,
commitment and faithfulness between God the Father and
Jesus Christ are simply beyond our comprehension. There
is a devotion to one another; to uphold each other in the
highest honor. This is more than we can imagine since our
own love for each other often falls far short compared to the
love of divinity. The Father has glorified the Son as the Son
has glorified the Father. The Father gives all power to the
Son and the Son gives all authority to the Father. The
Father tells us to listen to the Son, the Son tells us to listen
to the Father. The Son does nothing without the Father; the
Father only works through the Son. The Son tells us to
worship the Father, the Father tells us to worship the Son.
On and on we could go! The Father has given His all to the
Son and the Son has given His all to the Father. The only

way that God could possibly explain their relationship is by comparing the bond of love in human terms between a loving father and a loving son. Even this falls far short of the divine love that is within the Godhead. God has never called an angel His son, or any other spiritual being. However, through the redemption in Christ Jesus we are called, sons and daughters.

Romans 8:29
For whom He foreknew, He predestined to be the image of His Son, that He might be the firstborn among many brethren.

Jesus is clearly the *firstborn* of the *brethren,* not the firstborn of all creation, since not all the creation is called the *brethren.* The brethren are those who have been predestined, known before the foundations of the world, which are to be conformed to the likeness of the *firstborn,* Jesus Christ. *The brethren,* the ones who have accepted the sacrifice through faith are the many to follow in the resurrected power of God.

John 1:12 & 13
But as many as received Him, to them He gave the right to become children of God, to those who believe in His name: who were born, not of blood, nor of the will of man, but by God.

Faith in Jesus Christ entitles us to inherit the family positions as sons and daughters of God. Not because we have been born into an earthly vessel, but rather because we have been born from above following the *firstborn* of many, Jesus Christ, the *firstborn from the dead.*

The Only Savior

Isaiah 45:2
And there is no other god besides Me, a righteous God and
Savior; there is none besides me.
Hosea 13:4
...You know no God but Me, and besides Me there is no
savior.

God made it clear to the prophets of old that there is no
other god, no other savior besides Him. God is not willing to
share that title with anyone else since He states, *"There is*
none besides Me." No other god, no other savior, no other,
but He alone is the *Giver and Sustainer of all life*. And on an
ordinary night, through ordinary people, God's presence as
the only Savior was manifested in the flesh as a man. Yes,
He came to reveal the very heart of God to His beloved
creation, but the real mission was to save His finest
workmanship, which was created in His own image, from the
error of sin. Man had been diagnosed with a spiritual
terminal disease called sin, with only one possible cure, a
Savior, a final blood offering for the atonement of sin, and
His name is Jesus Christ. We certainly have something
special to celebrate, for through faith in His name we have
been given the gift of eternal life, the forgiveness of sins
through an everlasting covenant, from a faithful promise into
eternity.
  Let us give glory, honor and praise to *God our Savior.*

Luke 2:11
For there is born to you this day in the city of David a Savior,
who is Christ the Lord.

The New Testament writers proclaimed the birth of the
Savior, who is Christ the Lord. However, we read in the
opening Scriptures, through the prophet Isaiah how God told
him that there is no other god or savior except for Him. God
repeats this throughout the Old Testament.

Isaiah 49:26
All flesh shall know that I, the Lord, am your Savior, And
your Redeemer, the Mighty One of Jacob.

So who is the real Savior? Does God the Father proclaim
that there is no other savior except for Him? The angels who
stand in the very presence of God point to Jesus as our
Savior. However, the Apostle Paul clearly states that God is
our Savior'

1ˢᵗ Timothy 1:1
Paul, an apostle of Jesus Christ, by the commandment of
God our Savior and the Lord Jesus Christ our Hope.

We know that there are no contradictions in the word of
God. Therefore, we can only come to one explanation as to
why God the Father and His Son both hold the title as
Savior of the world. Peter gives us the answer

2ⁿᵈ Peter 1:1 & 11
To those who have obtained like precious faith with us by
the righteousness of our God and Savior Jesus Christ.
For so an entrance will be supplied to you abundantly into
the everlasting kingdom of our Lord and Savior Jesus Christ.

In the above Scriptures we receive an explanation through
the words of the Holy Spirit clearly testifying the deity of
Christ. We can rest assure that God is our only Savior, God
the Father and God the Son are in complete unity, therefore
they are two, yet they are one. For the Three, share the title
as One. Father, Son and Holy Spirit.
The Pharisees knew what Jesus was claiming right from the
beginning. The Apostle John gives us a true description of
what the religious leaders were in an uproar about, based
on the testimony of Christ in His own words.

John 5:18
Therefore, the Jews sought to kill Him, because He not only broke the Sabbath, but also said that God was His Father, making Himself equal to God.
John 10:33
The Jews answered Him, saying, "For a good work we do not stone You, but for blasphemy, and because You, being a Man, make Yourself God."

The religious leaders were not imagining the words of deity as Jesus clearly told them who He is. Jesus claimed to be the Son of God. We must remember that the Jews were defending the Law of Moses. They knew that the law came from God and was given to God's own chosen people to help them recognize sin and depart from it, or deal with judgment. They knew the law, yet they did not know the one who gave it to them, who was standing right in front of them. We read how John the Baptist recognized Jesus as soon as He began to walk toward him. We read how the three wise men bowed down before the Infant Jesus and worshipped Him, recognizing His deity. Anna, the prophetess knew who Jesus was as soon as Mary and Joseph walked in with the Infant. We read about a man named Simeon, who also recognized the Infant Jesus as soon as he laid his eyes on Him. So why did the religious leaders not see Jesus for who He is? It is obvious that they were looking in the wrong place. They knew the words of the Scriptures, but were unable to identify the one who spoke them. They were spiritually shortsighted, unable to see beyond their own pride, darkened by sin. God told them repeatedly that He is their only Savior, and that He would disarm the true enemy and save them.

Isaiah 63: 8 & 62: 11
Therefore, He became their Savior. In all their affliction, He was afflicted.
'Surely your salvation is coming; Behold, His reward is with Him.'

Throughout the Scriptures of old, we read the promise of a Savior, a Christ, the Holy Anointed One to come and take on Himself the sins of the people. So, why then did the religious leaders of the Jews, to whom the promise was given, not believe His testimony? Prophecy was being fulfilled right before their eyes; the very words that they studied for years were actually taking place before them. Jesus gave a testimony to the disciples of John the Baptist when John, who was now sitting in a prison cell, began to doubt the completion of his mission. John sends messengers to bring him back a conformation from Jesus. This alone is a very powerful lesson in that a man like John the Baptist, who was called to lead the charge for the mission of Christ, fell as a victim to doubt. Nevertheless, Jesus gives his disciples a clear message, one that John would no doubt understand, one that the religious leaders of the Jews should have also recognized.

Luke 7: 22
Jesus answered and said to them, "Go tell John the things you have seen and heard: that the blind see; the lame walk, the lepers are cleansed, the deaf hear, the dead are raised, the poor have the gospel preached to them.

Jesus was telling the disciples of John that prophecy was being fulfilled and that John indeed completed his mission. So, why was the religious leaders blinded to the prophecy that they had studied for years?

Psalm 25: 14
The secret of the Lord is with those who fear Him, and He will show them His covenant.

God gives us the answer through the Apostle Paul on why the hidden mystery, the secret of the Lord was not found by the religious leaders of that day. They were the ones who should have recognized Him as Lord and Savior, but instead, they did not know Him.

1ˢᵗ Corinthians 2: 14
But the natural man does not receive the things of the Spirit of God, for they are foolishness to him: nor can he know them, because they are spiritually discerned.

The natural man will resist, and even at times will wage war against the principles of faith. For faith is born in the spirit of a man and not in the natural. The Scriptures remind us that Jesus is the Author and Finisher of our faith. Without faith, we are simply blind to the things of the Spirit, which was the case in these religious leaders. These leaders knew the law and they knew the rituals of the law, but they had no faith, therefore they remained spiritually blind to the fact that the Savoir of all humanity had entered the natural world. Paul goes on to describe the principles of faith as a mystery to the natural mind, a hidden wisdom, hidden in the spirit of men and women. For it is in our spirits that Jesus is revealed as Lord and Savior, and King of all kings.

1ˢᵗ Corinthians 2: 7 & 8
But we speak the wisdom of God in a mystery, the hidden wisdom which God ordained before the ages for our glory, which none of the rulers of this age knew; for if they had known, they would have not crucified the Lord of Gory.

Paul had no doubt who his Savior was. He confirms this repeatedly in the letters written to churches that he had helped established. Paul makes no error in declaring that God is his Savior.

Timothy 1: 1 & 4:10
Paul, an apostle of Jesus Christ, by the commandment of God our Savior...

For to this end we both labor and suffer reproach, because we trust in the living God, who is the Savior of all men, especially of those who believe.

Titus 1: 3
... According to the commandment of God our Savior.

The apostle clearly identifies God as the one and only Savior for all men as did the prophets of old. In the above Scripture, he is giving Timothy clear pastoral instruction on sound doctrine. Paul goes on to identify Jesus as our Savior.

Titus 1: 4, Philippians 3: 20
Grace, mercy and peace from God the Father and the Lord Jesus Christ our Savior.
For our citizenship is in heaven, from which we also eagerly wait for the Savior, the Lord Jesus Christ.

The Apostle Paul, who probably did more to preach the word of God to the Gentiles then some of the old prophets did to preach the word of God to the Jews, names Jesus as his Savior. He was well aware of the Old Testament promises and commands given to the prophets as to God being the only Savior. Paul who was one of those religious leaders who had studied the Scriptures knew the law and the judgment for worshipping anyone or anything besides God. When Paul declared his faith in a written testimony, confessing Jesus as his Savior, he knew exactly what his commitment meant in the eyes of those who were blind to the truth. After all, Paul at one time was one of them; he led the attack on those who believed. There is no miss-interpretation as Paul clearly gives devoted, reverent honor to Jesus as the Savior of mankind. We see the other disciples testify in the same Spirit of devotion that God is our Savior

2nd Peter 1: 1
To those who have obtained like precious faith with us by the righteousness of our God and Savior Jesus Christ.

The Good Shepherd

John 10: 11
"I am the Good Shepherd. The Good Shepherd gives His life for the Sheep."

Jesus gives us a clear insight of His position, His deity and His love for us in the illustration of how a shepherd cares, provides and leads his sheep. This is a hard concept for us westerners to follow, since most of us have no real experience with herding sheep. This illustration was perfect for the many shepherds in the days of Christ to associate with what Jesus was teaching them about Himself. Jesus repeatedly associated with common occupations such as farming, building and even herding when teaching about the kingdom of God. Many of us can associate with building something, whether a model, a car, home improvement and many other projects that might come our way as a homeowner, or through hobbies. Many of us have done some kind of planting, whether it was houseplants, a vegetable garden, or flowers to beautify our surroundings. However, when it comes to sheep herding, we lose insight very quickly on the example Jesus gives reference to who He is as a Shepherd.

John 10:14
"I am the Good Shepherd; and I know My sheep, and am known by my own."

Again, in the same chapter we hear Jesus reveal Himself as the *Good Shepherd*. Before we can really understand what Jesus is telling us about His identity, we need to understand the job responsibilities of a shepherd. The main job description for a shepherd is to protect the sheep. We also need to understand the advanced mentality of a sheep and their weapons of defense, none!
Above all, sheep are one of the dumbest animals to walk the face of the earth. Ants have more intelligence then sheep. Sheep have no sense in working together like an ant. They

are unable to organize themselves in any type of formation, like the ant. Ants have the amazing ability to coordinate and organize their work efforts as a unit to accomplish their objectives. Have you ever seen sheep do that? Even an ant has the ability to help another ant in trouble. An ant will carry a fellow ant in time of need. A sheep will only make a poor attempt to run in fear at the first sign of any trouble. Sheep are so dumb that if one walks off a cliff, the rest will follow. I wish that Jesus had called me an ant instead of a sheep. Moreover, when it comes to a sheep protecting itself, they are really in trouble. They do not have large teeth to bite their enemies. They do not have large claws to rip the enemies flesh open. They cannot even run that fast! In other words, sheep have no defense against an enemy.

Now, in the natural, this is something that can really damage our egos, that Jesus is calling us sheep! One could take this as an insult, as one being dumb and weak. After all, I thought God said He loved us! However, we need to understand that Jesus is not talking about our natural state, but rather our spiritual reality. In the spiritual realm, we are easy prey for our enemy through the deception of our minds. Therefore, our minds are easily deceived by the lies of the enemy, which will result in a spiritual and mental headlock that will eventually choke the life right out of us. Are we that dumb and weak in the spiritual realm? Let me put it this way, a loin does not need a shepherd. A bear does not need a shepherd. Jesus compares us to sheep and sheep need a shepherd. The world is in the current chaotic state of evil that prevails in the heart of many because they have no shepherd and they certainly need one.

On the other hand, Satan is referred to as a stranger, a thief and a robber, a wolf that wants to steal, kill and destroy the sheep. Therefore, we can see why we need a shepherd, since we do have an enemy. Why are we so weak in the spiritual realm? Why do we not have the capabilities to destroy Satan's consistent attacks on our lives without the protection of the Shepherd?

Without mentioning his name, there was a President of the United States, who was often seen falling asleep in church. His wife finally approached him in anger and demanded to know how he could keep falling asleep during the service. The President replied, "I heard every word that was preached, the pastor spoke about sin, sin and sin." As humorous as this might seem, sin had stripped us of the authority that we once had. Jesus, the Great Shepherd has taken back the authority that Adam had so carelessly given away to a fallen angel. We now have the authority through His faithfulness, through His strength, through His power and through His promises.

Psalm 23: 1
The Lord is my shepherd...

A young shepherd boy, who became a hero and then a king, gives us one of the greatest insights of the Good Shepherd. This young boy had some real experiences out in the pasture while protecting his flock of sheep. He later uses these to relate to the protection of God in our lives. The young boy had spent day after day in the fields, singing and worshiping God while overseeing the responsibility that was entrusted to him. As any other good shepherd, his responsibility was to protect the sheep. We heard the story many times about a young shepherd boy who stands up to a giant monster of a man with nothing more that a small sling shot and some very big faith. Where did this boy receive such faith? He was not a priest, or a religious leader in the church. The boy received such faith, to bring down the demonic monster through worshiping God, even out in the pasture. Why did this boy have so much confidence in God? He tells us while he stands before his enemy.

1st Samuel 17: 37
Moreover David said, "The Lord, who delivered me from the paw of the lion and from the paw of the bear, He will deliver me from the hand of the Philistine (Goliath)."

David had some real faith experiences. He understood his job responsibilities as a shepherd; therefore, he was able to relate to God's promises of protection, as God is bound by His word. This young shepherd boy, through God's word and faith experiences, knew that God is the *Shepherd and Overseer of our souls.*

1ˢᵗ Peter 2: 25
For you were like sheep going astray, but have now returned to the Shepherd and Overseer of your souls.

The lion and the bear had come to the pasture were David was herding his sheep. David gives the Philistine (Goliath) and us an account of how God, being the Good Shepherd, delivered the young boy from the beast. We do not know the full details, but I can assure you that David knew who to call when trouble came into camp. The boy as a shepherd, worshipped God as his Shepherd, for he knew that God takes care of what belongs to Him, just as the young boy had taken his responsibility seriously to care for and protect his flock. The Philistine falls by faith in the hands of a young shepherd boy who knew who his Shepherd was. Do you have any beast attacking you today?   Do you have any giant monsters threatening to end your career, your marriage, your ministry or your children's lives? Who is the Shepherd that David had so much faith in? Who is it that Peter referrers to as the Shepherd and Overseer of our souls?

John 10:11 & 14
"I am the Good Shepherd. The Good Shepherd gives His life for the sheep."
"I am the Good Shepherd; and I know my sheep and am known by my own."

Jesus is the *Shepherd and Overseer of our souls.* He is the one who already has taken out the teeth of the loin, and declawed the paws of the bear. He has already crushed the head of the giant monster (Satan), who has threatened us with empty lies. Jesus has taken the responsibility of the Shepherd, and as any good shepherd will tell you, the main objective of the shepherd is to protect the sheep! If we are willing to receive Jesus Christ as our Savoir, our Protector, our Shepherd, then we need not worry about the loin, the bear or the giant monsters in our lives. We have a Great Shepherd, our Protector. Moreover, one of the greatest things about this Shepherd is the He also became a sheep, an unblemished lamb who has already rescued us from the enemy of sin by His own blood. Even when He took the form of a sheep, He never ceased being the Great Shepherd.

Philippians 2:6, 7
Who, being in the form of God, did not consider it robbery to be equal with God, but made Himself of no reputation, taking the form of a bondservant, and coming in the likeness of a man.

Our Great Shepherd does not only protect us; He leads us with a sure guidance to green pastures and still waters.

Psalm 23:2
He makes me to lie down in green pastures; He leads me beside the still waters.

Jesus brings us to a place of renewing, a place of refreshing, and a place of His peace. The secondary objective of the Shepherd toward His flock is to lead them into a place of safety where fear has no place in their lives. A place of assurance where doubt is swallowed up by faith, hate is overcome by love and death is defeated by life. The Good Shepherd knows the safest place for His flock is a place of rest. Although, we must be willing to follow and trust Him as the sheep trust their shepherd, for the Shepherd knows what is best for the sheep. I was with my brother on a horse farm one day, when I began to realize the true value of one horse compared to another. I am not very knowledgeable about horses, but by listening to the conversations of the experienced riders, God revealed to me a value in these great animals and in us. The experienced riders were not as interested in color, the strength or the size of the horse. They seemed to evaluate the horse by his obedience, his ability to obey a command. The horses that obeyed the best were of the most value to these riders. Is our obedience a value to God? If we are willing to follow the Shepherd, obey His instruction and rest in His love; then goodness and mercy will follow us all the days of our lives. However, this is not our natural state.

Isaiah 53:6
All we like sheep have gone astray; we have turned, every one, to his own way...

We are referred to as sheep that have not followed the Shepherd, sheep that have gone astray, the lost sheep. We have all followed our own path in some time of our lives. Searching for our own justification and self-righteousness, we have danced to the beat of our own drum. However, God did not interfere with our decision, but let us go our own way. Moreover, while drifting farther away from God, we found ourselves unprotected and easy prey for the predator to devour

1ˢᵗ Peter 5:8
Be sober; be vigilant; because your adversary the devil walks about like a roaring loin, seeking whom he may devour.

Our natural thinking will lead us astray, unprotected into the claws of our enemy. As a sheep that had traveled away from the flock and the protection of the shepherd, so are we that have gone our own course, and then wonder why we are shipwrecked off the coast of an unknown Island. Many people may put on a good show, a mask of contentment, and the make-up of peace and security. Many might say that all is well, but the true inner peace of God is absent from their lives, as it was in mine. I could not recognize it, I was so far away from the flock that I could no longer see the Shepherd, but I knew that I was missing the peace of God's protection. An unprotected sheep that no longer has the protection and guidance of the Shepherd will end up in dangerous territory every time. The Holy Spirit reveals to the Prophet Isaiah our natural state, and God reminds the Apostle Peter and us not to return there once we have been united with the Shepherd. For in the presence of the Shepherd there is protection and safety. Moreover, the peace of God lives in the hearts of the flock that follows the Shepherd, since they are no longer plagued by uncertainty, but now know the voice of Him who calls them.

John 10: 27
My sheep hear my voice, and I know them, and they follow me.

The Lord Jesus begins to teach us about a relationship; the one that we need to have with Him. What is a relationship and how does in work? We all know that there are many types of relationships, from the very swallow ones like the simple hello and goodbye, to the deep relationships that we have with our family members. Which one do you think God is interested in sharing with us? Can we have a relationship with anybody without conversation? Can we know anyone in a deep relationship without exchanging words? Relationships begin and are sustained in two-way conversations. God is not an exception to this rule. Take out the communication in any relationship and the relationship will be very shallow, or will disappear altogether. The Lord Jesus tells us that we will hear His voice. We cannot hear and recognize His voice if we have no relationship with Him. How many times do we pick up the telephone to hear a voice that we cannot recognize, someone we have a shallow relationship with, or have not spoken with for a long time? Why cannot we hear God? Can we recognize the voices of those with whom we have deep relationships? Some religions state that God will only speak to us through His word. God does speak to us through His word, but the Lord said we would know His voice as well. The reason why the world cannot hear His voice is simply because, they do not know Him within a deep relationship. Without a two-way communication in any relationship, there is no relationship at all. Try not communicating with your wife or husband, your children or your parents, even your boss and co-workers for a long time and see what happens. God speaks to us through His word and our spirits because of who He is. Jesus is our Shepherd, who cares for us with an undying love. He was willing to lay His life down for the sheep and canceled the charge that was held against us. Jesus also reminds Peter that we will see Him again if we abide in the protection of His love and follow Him to the streets of glory.

1st Peter 5: 4
And when the Chief Shepherd appears, you will receive the crown of glory that does not fade away.

David, the shepherd boy turned king, did not know Jesus in the flesh as Peter did, however; he knew Him through his spirit. David knew the Lord Jesus as his Shepherd and Savior in the field and in the palace.
Another man is met by the Shepherd on a Damascus road and he decides to follow the Shepherd and feed His flock.

Hebrews 13: 20
Now may the God of peace who brought up our Lord Jesus from the dead, that Great Shepherd of the sheep, through the blood of the everlasting covenant, make you complete in every good work to do His will, working in you what is well pleasing in His sight, through Jesus Christ, to whom be the glory forever and ever. Amen.

We see Jesus proclaim repeatedly that He is the Good Shepherd, the Shepherd who has searched out the lost sheep of Israel, and then the other nations of the world. We see the apostles all point to Jesus as the Great Shepherd of the flock. We see God speak to Ezekiel concerning His flock and He being the Shepherd.

Ezekiel 34:11 & 12
'For thus says the Lord: "Indeed I Myself will search for My sheep and seek them out. As a shepherd seeks out his flock on the day he is among his scattered sheep, so I will seek out My sheep and deliver them from all places where they were scattered on a cloudy and dark day."

God tells the prophet: *"As a shepherd among his sheep, I Myself will search for My sheep."* God did come among His sheep as one of them. God visited mankind in the form of a man. Through the natural laws came Jesus Christ. God repeatedly refers to His people as His flock, His possession. He does not share this with anyone else; He takes soul possession and responsibility as any good shepherd would. We can also see in the Gospel of John that Jesus takes possession and full responsibility for His sheep just as God told the prophet Ezekiel.

Ezekiel 34:31
"You are My flock, the flock of My pasture; you are men, and I am your God," says the Lord God.

John 10:11, 14, 27
"I (Jesus) am the Good Shepherd. The Good Shepherd gives His life for the sheep."
"I (Jesus) am the Good Shepherd; and I know My sheep, and am known be My own."
"My sheep hear My voice, and I (Jesus) know them, and they follow Me."

Jesus tells us that we are His possession. We belong to Him if we believe that He is our Lord and Savoir, God the Son, to the glory of God the Father. Jesus tells us that He knows us and if we belong to Him, we will know His voice. We can hear the voice of God with our spiritual ears, but without ears, in the natural or in the spiritual, we are deaf. Therefore, Jesus tells His flock, His people that if we really know Him, we will hear His voice because we are His. As the sheep in the pasture knows the shepherd who directs them, protects them, brings them to a place of safety and security and feeds them what they need, so is Jesus to those who believe on His name. Our Shepherd, Jesus Christ is dedicated, and committed to His sheep, all that believe on His name, and no one can steal one of His sheep from Him.

John 10: 28
"I (Jesus) *give them eternal life, and they shall never perish, neither shall anyone snatch them out of My hand."*

Jesus is the Great Shepherd as God the Son is committed to the purpose of God the Father, as the Holy Spirit is committed to both, the Three are One. The Scriptures clearly reveal to us the commitment with in the Godhead, the complete unity of God. Every word, every command, every blessing and every warning comes from the heart of the God the Father, through Jesus Christ. Jesus tells us repeatedly that whoever receives Him, whoever believes in Him, whoever serves Him, whoever acts on His word; receives, believes and serves the Father. Therefore, those who believe in the Son are also in unity with the unified commitment within the Godhead.

John 13:20, 15:23, 14:9
"Most assuredly, I (Jesus) *say to you, he who receives whomever I send receives Me, and he who receives Me receives Him who sent Me."*

Jesus answered and said to him, "If anyone loves Me, he will keep My word: and my Father will love him, and We will come to him and make Our home with him."

"He who has seen Me (Jesus) has seen the Father."

Jesus reveals the total unification within God and the commitment and faithfulness toward one another, even through the obedience of Christ to God the Father, giving Himself for the redemption of mankind as the eternal sacrifice. Jesus reveals this divine unity and goes a step further; He invites us to enter into their love as an orphan child would enter into a loving faithful family. God has extended His hand of love, faithfulness and commitment toward us; our only requirement is faith in Him, the Good Shepherd, Jesus Christ.

I AM

Exodus 3:13
Then Moses said to God, "Indeed, when I come to the
children of Israel and say to them, 'The God of your fathers
has sent me to you,' and they say to me, 'What is His
name?' What shall I say to them?"

Moses brings a question to God, that up until that point in
history, no one had asked, except Jacob. Adam had never
asked that question, or Abraham never asked that question.
No one except Jacob ever asked if God had a name. Was it
important to Adam or Abraham? Moreover, it appears that if
Moses had never asked the question, God did not consider
it important enough to mention. Why was not it important to
Adam or Abraham?

And God said to Moses, "I AM WHO I AM."

This is a very interesting response from God. The fact that
God had no intentions of giving Moses a revelation of His
name, and His unusual response to the question gives us a
good indication on God's thoughts on the subject. God was
really telling Moses, 'I Am Me.' *"I Am Who I Am."* Was God
telling Moses that Adam, Abraham and Isaac did not need a
name to place their faith in Him?
Nevertheless, God agrees to a name, and the name is
simply, *I AM.* If a name was going to help the Israelites weak
faith, then God was more than willing to accommodate the
request. After all, it was a request that Moses clearly asked
God, for the sole purpose of giving the people of Israel a
more intimate encounter with the Divine. These people were
weak in faith. They had been in bondage with recent
hardships; although, they were treated with respect for many
years while they were living in Egypt and prospered in many
ways.

Exodus 1: 7
But the children of Israel were fruitful and increased
abundantly, multiplied and grew exceedingly mighty: and the
land was filled with them.

There should be no question that God's blessing were upon
these people. They *increased abundantly, multiplied and*
grew exceedingly mighty. Notice the key words that the Holy
Spirit gives to describe their success. They *abundantly*
increased and were *exceedingly mighty.* In other words,
they were abundantly and exceedingly successful. Any
shareholder would be well pleased to see those words
describing the growth of his or her investment on a financial
report. The people who had been chosen as God's very own
were living in the prosperity of His blessing. Of course, there
was only one problem with this scenario; they were
prospering in someone else's land. Usually, in times of great
blessing comes a real test of faith. There are times when we
could easily begin to place our trust in the blessings, instead
of in the one who gives them.
Also, keep in mind that God had a lot of work to do with
these people in establishing their faith. They had enjoyed
the blessing of God without really knowing Him.
Nevertheless, the favor of the Israelites began to turn when
a new king came into power. The king sees the Israelites as
a threat and not a blessing; therefore, he began to plan on
how to keep them down as slaves rather than co-workers.
Ever had someone turn the tables on you because they felt
that you were some kind of threat to them? This happens in
business all the time as managers use people to assure or
justify their positions. Unfortunately, when these things
happen to us we forget that hardships are really a test of
faith and will leave us in a better position then where we
were before. I know at the time when someone is making
your life difficult, it is not easy to think about the blessings
that will follow when passing a test of faith. God never said it
is easy.

Nevertheless, Moses is called to deliver these now persecuted people of God to the promise of living in their own land flowing with milk and honey. Now Moses, who was not raised with the teachings of the Israelites and who did not know God; is faced with a task of being the spokesmen for God and a vital tool in the release of God's chosen people. Moses did not know God, he did not know the people of Israel, and he did not know how all of this was going to fit together. Therefore, Moses explains to God that he needs something to bring to the people of Israel so they will believe him. Moses was confused in thinking that this task was going to be fulfilled by some power or some talent that he possessed. At this point Moses did not have the big picture. There are times when we also think like Moses, in that we assume that we will complete a task of faith or achieve a victory by our own power.

Exodus 3:11
But Moses said to God, "Who am I that I should go to Pharaoh, and that I should bring the children of Israel out of Egypt?"

It is interesting how we ask God the same question as Moses when we are faced with new challenges of faith. We automatically assume that we will face these problems alone and will have to rely on our own power and strength. God knew exactly where Moses was coming from and He reassures Moses that he will not be alone.

Exodus 3: 11
So He, (God) Said, "I will certainly be with you."

God tells us the same thing; it is our choice, to believe Him or not. God tells Moses that He will give him a sign so the people will believe that God had sent him. Moses is starting to come around, but he needs something more than promises, Moses needs a name. Moses needs something that he can go to the people and prove that he really did

speak with God. Now keep in mind, when God first
introduces Himself to Moses, He addresses Himself as the
God of the fathers.

Exodus 3: 6
Moreover, He said, "I am the God of your fathers, the God of
Abraham, the God of Isaac; the God of Jacob."

God does not mention any name, but simply introduces
Himself as God. That was enough for Adam, Abraham and
Isaac, although we will discover that the founding fathers did
indeed address God by a name, but not the same name that
was given to Moses. Nevertheless, Moses needed a name.
God tells Moses that if you need a name to convince the
people that I sent you, then I will give you a name, the name
given is *I AM*. God never expressed this name before, since
up until this time there was no need for God to be addresses
with a name. God simply accommodates Moses by
answering his prayer, although God still addresses Himself
as the God of the fathers even after the conversation with
Moses.

Exodus 3: 16
"Go and gather the elders of Israel together, and say to
them, 'The Lord God of your fathers, the God of Abraham, of
Isaac, and of Jacob, appeared to me...'

Now even when God did agree to a name so Moses would
have something to tell the children of Israel about his
encounter with Him, God uses a name that expresses His
eternal existence. God tells Moses that He is who He is.
This would be like someone asking your name and you reply
by saying, 'I am me.' It does not really answer the question,
but this is exactly how God answers Moses. Let us look at
some of the other names God calls Himself.

Isaiah 48:12, 48:10, 43:3, 54:5, 57:15, 63:16; Exodus 34:14;
Genesis 15: 2 & 8

"I am He, I am the First, I am also the Last."
"The Holy One of Israel: I am the Lord your God."
"For I am the Lord your God, the Holy One of Israel, your Savior."
The Lord of host is His name...
For thus says the High and lofty One Who inhabits eternity, whose name is Holy...
You, O Lord, are our Father; Our Redeemer from Everlasting is Your name.
"For you shall worship no other god, for the Lord, whose name is Jealous, is a jealous God."
And Abram said, "Lord God, what will you give me..."
And he said, "Lord God, how shall I know that I will inherit it?"

We can see that God addressed Himself with different names. God also tells us that He was known to Abraham as the Lord God, since it is not recorded that the name *I AM* was ever given to Abraham.

Exodus 6: 2 & 3
And God spoke to Moses and said to him, "I am the Lord, (YHWH, Jehovah) I appeared to Abraham, to Isaac, to Jacob as the God Almighty, but by My name, I AM, I was not known to them."

God is clearly telling us that Abraham, Isaac or Jacob did not know him by the name *I AM, YHWH,* (traditionally interpreted as Jehovah). However, He was known by a name, as we read that Abraham called on the name of the Lord,

Genesis 12:8
... He, (Abraham) *built an altar to the Lord and called on the name of the Lord.*

God clearly tells us that He was not known as *"I AM* "prior to the conversation with Moses. However, it is obvious that God was known to Abraham by a name.

Genesis 13: 4
...To the place of the alter which he, (Abraham) *had made there first. And there Abram,* (Abraham) *called on the name of the Lord.*

Abraham called on the name of the Lord. It does not say that God had given Abraham a specific name as He had done with Moses, but Abraham did have a name for God.

Genesis 26: 24 & 25
And the Lord appeared to him, (Isaac) *the same night and said, "I am the God of your father Abraham; do not fear, for I am with you. I will bless you and multiply your descendants for My servant Abraham's, sake." So he,* (Isaac) *built an altar there and called on the name of the Lord.*

Abraham and Isaac both called on the name of the Lord. What exactly was that name? The name that Abraham called on God was not the name that God had given to Moses. Abraham addresses God as the Lord, God Most High, the Possessor of heaven and earth.

Genesis 14: 22
But Abram, (Abraham) *said to the king of Sodom, "I have raised my hand to the Lord, God Most High, Possessor of heaven and earth."*

God does begin to reveal His nature to Abraham. As we read the 15th chapter of Genesis, in these conversations we can see how Abraham addressed God and how God reveals Himself.

Genesis 15: 1 & 7
After these things the word of the Lord came to Abram in a
vision, saying, "Do not be afraid, Abram. I am your shield,
your exceedingly great reward."
Then He (God), said to him (Abraham), "I am the Lord, who
brought you out of Ur and the Chaldeans, to give you the
land to inherit it?"

God does begin to reveal His protective nature and the fact
that He is the greatest gift we could ever receive.
On another occasion, we read about a slave woman who
had belonged to Abraham and she calls on the name of the
Lord.

Genesis 16: 13
The she called the name of the Lord who spoke to her, You-
Are-the-God-Who-Sees-All; (Hebrew EL ROI) for she said...

We also read about Jacob, who wrestled with a Man until
daybreak, and would not let go of Him until the Man blessed
him.

Genesis 32:17
Then Jacob was left alone; and a Man wrestled with him
until the breaking of the day.

Then Jacob has his name changed to Israel, the same way
God changed Abram's name to Abraham, and receives a
blessing from God, the same way Abraham did. However, in
the conversation, Jacob asked His name. This is interesting
because, if Jacob knew the name of God, a name that
would have been handed down from Abraham to Isaac, why
would he have asked for another name? For Jacob testifies
that he had seen God face to face.

Genesis 32: 32, 33
Then Jacob asked, saying, "Tell me Your name, I pray." And
He said, "Why is it that you ask about My name?" And He
blessed him there. So Jacob called the place Face of God:
"For I have seen God face to face, and my life is preserved."

Jacob did not receive an answer to his question, but
receives a question for a question. We have seen God
respond like this many times in the Scriptures. In any event,
no name was given to Jacob. God does appear to Jacob
again and this time God introduces Himself as God
Almighty.

Genesis 35: 11
And God said to him, (Jacob): I am the God Almighty.

We know that God did respond to different names. As we
will read later on, God does give us a name that will get His
attention every time it is used in faith and according to His
will.
Moving into the New Covenant, we see that Jesus
addresses God as Father. Why would He not? How many
sons who honor and respect their fathers would address
their fathers by their names? That would be disrespectful
even from a human viewpoint. Jesus shares with us the
intimate, loving, holy relationship within the Godhead.
When reading the gospels we must understand that Jesus
was once pure Spirit with no outer shell of natural flesh. The
Apostle John gives us a great revelation at the very
beginning of his gospel of the pre-existence and deity of
Jesus Christ.
John: 1 & 14
In the beginning was the Word (Jesus), and the Word
(Jesus), was with God, and the Word (Jesus), was God.
And the Word (Jesus) became flesh and dwelt among us,
and we beheld His glory...

When Jesus was pure Spirit in the Godhead, before His coming in the flesh, He is called, *'the Word'*. The apostle sets the foundation of his gospel in beginning his revelation from God on the identity and deity of Jesus Christ. He wasted no time in establishing Jesus as God the Son. These verses unmistakably show the eternal deity of Jesus. Jesus is given the praise as God!

As we read on in the gospel, John records the conversation between Jesus and the Pharisees that again reveals His eternal existences

John 8:53
"Are you greater than our father Abraham, who is dead? And the prophets are dead. Who do You make Yourself out to be?"

The Pharisees (the Jews), question the statements of Christ, and bring Abraham into the picture. A few verses back we read how the Jews were boasting on how they were descendants of Abraham and had been enslaved to no one. What the Jews were really saying was, 'we have faith in the fathers, for we know God spoke to them.' Therefore, after throwing Abraham's name around; as if they were trying to impress someone, Jesus wasted no time in telling them that Abraham was a witness to Him.

John 8: 56
"Your father Abraham rejoiced to see my day, and he saw it and was glad."

This brings the conversation to a new level, after all, Abraham was a witness to God, and he was *called a friend of God*. Therefore, now the defenses really start to go up. They just asked Jesus if He thought that He was greater than Abraham, the father of their religion, the father of their country, the one who was a *friend of God*. Jesus responses in not only saying that He is greater than Abraham, the father of the nation, but also that Abraham received a revelation of Him and was full of joy over it. We can well imagine that by now the conversation is getting heated, to say the least. The Jews now attempt to make sense of these words by asking Jesus another question that will result in revealing the identity of Jesus.

John 8:57
Then the Jews said to Him (Jesus), *"You are not yet fifty years old, and you have seen Abraham?"*

Confused by the words of Christ, the Jews attempt to reason with Him by rationalizing that Abraham lived long before, so how could He say that He saw Abraham? A logical approach to a claim that bewildered these Jews, as they could not grasp what Jesus was revealing to them. Therefore, to answer their question, Jesus reveals His identity.

John 8:58
Jesus said to them, "Most assuredly I say to you, before Abraham was, I AM."

Could Jesus have been the one who spoke to Moses? Is Jesus the one who has communicated with man from the Godhead from the very beginning, even from the Garden of Eden? Jesus makes a claim here that cannot be ignored, or mutilated into meaning something else. This is what God was telling Moses! God is beyond the limitations of time, beyond our logic, beyond our shallow understanding of what we perceive what God should be. God's response to Moses was the same response that Jesus told these questioning rulers as they tried to comprehend who He was and still is. If Jesus were only a man, this confession would be blasphemy, a sin and subject to death by being stoned under the law given to Moses. This statement was a direct confession of deity, since this was the name that the Jews used to identify God. The response of the Jews was one that should be expected, since they did not believe that Jesus was the Christ, the Savoir, God the Son.

John 8:59
Then they took up stones to throw at Him...

According to the law of Moses, this was grounds for being stoned to death, a Man claiming to be God. As we can read further on, the Jews wanted to stone Jesus on other occasions for this very reason.

John 10: 33
The Jews answered Him (Jesus), *saying, "For a good work we do not stone You, but for blasphemy, and because You, being a Man, make Yourself God."*

John 5: 8
Therefore, the Jews sought all the more to kill Him, because He not only broke the Sabbath, but also said that God was His Father, making Himself equal to God.

The Jewish teachers, the custodians for God, the experts of the law were ready to stone Jesus because they understood His claims to deity. They were blind to the truth; nevertheless, they understood His words as blasphemy against the God of their fathers. There is no question that the Jews understood the claims by Jesus concerning His identity. Jesus holds no truth back from the Jews as He continues to show His nature as God. Jesus is not claiming to be God the Father, but rather the second person within the Godhead, God the Son. Jesus goes on to give us a full view of His identity.

John 10: 30 7 31
"I and the Father are one."
Then the Jews took up stones to stone Him.

God the Father and God the Son are one, in complete unity, in complete harmony, in complete agreement as the Father loves the Son and the Son loves the Father. They are one in purpose, in truth and in love as God.
As we read on in the gospel, we see the gentle Jesus explaining to the Apostle Philip that He is in complete, eternal co-existence with the Father and anyone who receives Him receives the Father as well.

John 14: 8 & 9
Philip said to Him, "Lord show us the Father, and that will be sufficient for us." Jesus said to him, "Have I been with you so long, and yet you have not known Me, Philip? He who has seen Me has seen the Father; so how can you say, 'show us the Father?'"

Jesus left the throne of the Godhead to become a Man, on a search and rescue mission to save a dying humanity. He was Spirit, but was willing to put on an outer shell of flesh, and was willing to be subject to all the natural laws as we know them, including death. He is no longer a Spirit only, but He is a Man, glorified and sits at the right hand of the Father. There is now a Man in the Godhead! Jesus is the *I AM* from the Old Testament. He spoke to the prophets of old and revealed the mercy and judgment of God.

John 12: 44 & 45, 13: 20
Then Jesus cried out and said, "He who believes in Me, believes not in Me, but Him who sent Me. And he who sees Me sees Him who sent Me.
And he who receives Me receives Him who sent Me."

To believe in Jesus, to see Jesus, (with spiritual eyes), to receive Jesus, is to believe, see and receive God the Father. It is the name of Jesus that gives us access to the Throne of God. There is no other name given, no other name to proclaim the Savior of man.

Romans 2: 9
Therefore God also has highly exalted Him and given Him a name which is above every name, that at the name of Jesus every knee should bow, of those in heaven, and those on the earth, and of those under the earth.

We have been given a name that gives all that believe access to the mercy seat of God. Abraham and Moses did not have the name we now possess. They had to stand before God with their sin. God the Father has given His Son a name, *which is above every name,* and *every knee* will *bow* before that name. Even now, every demon that is an enemy against God must bow their ugly knee at the sound of His name when used in faith.

Acts 4:12
"Nor is there salvation in any other, for there is no other name under heaven given among men by which we must be saved."

It is the name of Jesus, which has the redeeming power, and that is able to remove the stain of our sin from our spirits. It is the name of Jesus that has been given for man's salvation, which no other name has been given. Although He is called by many other names, Jesus is the name, that when used in faith, will bring every evil spirit down to the knees.

Matthew 1: 23
"Behold, the virgin shall be with child and bear a Son, and they shall call His name Immanuel," which translated, "God with us"

The Teacher

1ˢᵗ Timothy 5:17
The elders who direct the affairs of the church are well worthy of double honor, especially those whose work is preaching and teaching.

We find many teachers that teach everything from cooking to computers. In every school or university, teachers instruct students. They teach their logic, their formulas, and their reasons of why they believe what they teach. They teach on what they have researched, striving to find the hidden answers to so many questions. Questions that sends their minds to finding an answer or a solution based on science, the principle laws of nature and what they have been taught. All the things that people have spent a lifetime in teaching will vanish; it will not help when it is time to leave here. God does want us to have knowledge in all that He has made, but the greatest knowledge, the most important knowledge we need to gain comes from knowing the Teacher of all teachers. The only knowledge that will matter is whether you know Him or not. When we stand before the Creator, there is no science, no theories, and no formulas; there is only God.

Here we see God give honor where honor is due concerning the teachers of the church. God tells us that the teachers of the church are worthy of honor, not worthy of a little honor, God says, *"well worthy of double honor."* What praise from the Almighty God! Why does God say this? When a pastor is preaching and teaching the word of God from a pure heart, they honor God, because they are not teaching just to glorify themselves, but to glorify God. Now a man from the ruling body of the Jews decided to pay Jesus a visit to question His teaching. I am sure that Jesus was tested many more times then is recorded in the Scriptures, since Jesus had made some very bold statements concerning His identity and the corruption and hypocrisy of the rulers of that day. I am also sure that this man Nicodemus had carefully planned a questioner for Jesus to answer concerning who He is. Nevertheless, the ruler approaches Jesus with respect in calling Him teacher.

John 3: 2
This man (Nicodemus)*, came to Jesus by night and said to Him, 'Rabbi, we know that You are a teacher come from God; for no one can do these signs that You do unless God is with him."*

This whole conversation between Jesus and a ruler of the Jews is a great revelation on the new birth, God's love and the foundation of salvation. All these insights from this chapter should be bound in our hearts and minds. However, here we see a man that was part of the ruling class with no knowledge of these things. Nicodemus was trained and tutored in the Law of Moses and with that knowledge he ruled according to the law. He was also well educated and well respected by his position. However, whatever questions this man had in mind to ask Jesus were thrown out the window when Jesus tells him that he must be *born again* to enter in the Kingdom of God. Jesus began teaching this man as soon as he entered in the room. Was Jesus a teacher? We will see that Jesus spent a lot of His time teaching. Now keep in mind that in the days of Nicodemus, a teacher was a highly respected position. These rulers were also teachers of the law, experts in the law of God that used the law to govern the people. The Scriptures do not reveal to us that Jesus ever went to law school and earned a degree. Nevertheless, this ruler and graduate of law approached Jesus as a Teacher. Moreover, not just any teacher, but Jesus is addressed as a teacher that came from God. The apostle is careful to include this in the conversation because it will give us a more real revelation into the divinity of Christ, since Jesus taught from God.

John 13: 3
Jesus knowing that the Father had given all things into His hands, and that He had come from God and was going to God.

The phrase, come from God does not mean that Jesus was a messenger whom the Father had sent from one of His billions of angels. Anytime we read about an angel that was manifested in the presence of people, they do not claim to be from God. The angel Gabriel, who has made some appearances in the natural, introduces himself as one who stands in God presence.

Luke 1: 19
And the angel answered and said to him, I am Gabriel, who stands in the presence of God, and was sent to speak to you and bring you glad tidings."

Gabriel tells us that he *stands in the presence of God*; he does not say that he came forth from God. However, Jesus tells us He had come from God (the Godhead), and was returning to God. Furthermore, no angel ever addressed God as Father. This is an important distinction between Jesus and any other spiritual being.
It is also interesting why Nicodemus addresses Jesus as Teacher.

"No one can do these signs that you do unless God is with him."

Jesus did not only teach the word of God, He brought it to pass in the presence of all. When Jesus spoke a word, it happened as He said it. We read in Genesis how God spoke the word and brought forth creation. Nicodemus was obviously impressed with this type of teaching. Little did Nicodemus know that this was far more than just teaching, it was the manifest presence of the word of God? As the conversation goes on, and Jesus teaches the well- educated ruler about the fundamentals of the new birth, the ruler cannot grasp the revelation.

John 3: 9
Nicodemus answered and said to Him (Jesus), "How can these things be?"

The ruler, the teacher of the law is totally lost when it comes to the revelation of the re-birth of the spirit. Jesus leaves him in a wondering state of mind. Jesus asked him some very important questions that I believe will be asked to every religious teacher concerning the education of spiritual re-birth.

John 3:10
Jesus answered and said to him (Nicodemus), "Are you the teacher of Israel and do not know these things?"

The past, present and future religious leaders who do not teach the re-birth mandate of God, will certainly stand before the throne of the Lord and will be asked the same question. If I may paraphrase this question, Jesus was saying, 'Nicodemus, what have you been teaching?' Many religious leaders claim to teach the truth. They may have very promenade positions in a religious organization, but if they are not teaching the fundamentals of spiritual re-birth, they are not teachers of the truth, and will be held accountable as we see Nicodemus was.
As we read the Scriptures, we see that Jesus accepted many titles. They called Him *the Christ, the Messiah, the Son of God, the Son of Man, the Lord, The King, The Lamb of God* and last but not least, *the Teacher, (Rabbi).*

John 1:38, 1:49
They said to Him (Jesus), "Rabbi, where are you staying."
Nathaniel answered and said to Him (Jesus), "Rabbi, You are the Son of God! You are the King of Israel!"

Jesus accepted all the titles of deity, but He was also receptive to the position and title of teacher *(Rabbi)*. When we study the daily routine of Jesus, we will discover three positions of ministry that occupied most of His time.

He spent a lot of time in prayer, (sometimes all night). The Scriptures tell us that He would often leave His disciples at evening, go to a secluded place and pray until morning.

Jesus also spent lot of time healing people. We read how the multitudes came to Him for healing. The word about Him was spreading fast, and many with illness and sickness would come and seek healing. The Scriptures tell us about a house where Jesus was in that was so crowded, that certain men cut a whole in the roof to lower a sick man to Jesus for healing.

Jesus utilized the rest of His time teaching the people in spiritual principles. Jesus sat on a mountain, stood on a boat and visited the local temples to teach and preach the word of God throughout Israel.

Jesus took the position of teaching very seriously, as we can see to His response to Nicodemus when He clearly rebukes him for falling to understand and teach spiritual principles. Jesus enjoyed teaching; He enjoyed sharing His infinite knowledge with the creation that was birth through Him and for Him. He enjoyed teaching and proving the principles of faith and watching people being set free by what He taught. True teachers give of themselves. I have heard many preachers who claim to know something and teach for a reaction from the congregation. A true teacher is not looking for a reaction, but rather a change in the thinking patterns of their students, that will set them free from whatever holds them captive. I believe that teaching is certainly one of the highest callings of God for anyone who has been chosen to perform such an honored task. Jesus still enjoys teaching His creation.

Matthew 5: 1 & 2
And seeing the multitudes, He (Jesus), *went up to a mountain, and when He was seated His disciples came to Him. Then He opened His mouth and taught them...*

Whether there was a crowd or a single person, Jesus took the opportunity to teach people. He knew that they were victims of ignorance. We also can become so overwhelmed with our day-to-day problems that we often lose sight of God and become victims of doubt. Jesus understands our makeup. He sees our poor decisions due to our anxiousness, and our frail nerves when faced with pressure, even our unstable emotions that can travel from tears to anger in seconds. How can God truly understand all our elements? There is a saying in some parts of the world that says, 'don't criticize the man unless you have walked in his shoes.' God is not only the Creator of all life, but through the life of Jesus Christ, He became part of His creation. This should be an extremely comforting aspect of the believer's walk of faith. Jesus felt what we feel. He knew hunger, he felt pain; experienced betrayal, even from His friends. He cried, knowing the fate of the lost. He healed the sick out of His compassion, and taught as much as He could so to correct the misguided minds of those around Him.
I remember working as a manufacturing manager, and on the first day in a new company, I could see that there were some good employees working in the plant, but had been taught some bad habits. They were not bad employees, just misguided. I believe Jesus looks into our hearts from this viewpoint. For the teachings of Christ are life changing, and are still able to deliver us into the peace of God. His teachings are timeless, unaffected by the eras of man, unchanged by our seasons. For as Jesus lives, so His words live forever. He is the same today, as yesterday, and will be always, and so are His words.

Matthew 7: 28 & 29
So it was, when Jesus had ended these sayings, that the people were astonished at His teachings, for He taught them as one having authority, and not as the scribes.

Mark 1: 22
And they were astonished at His (Jesus), teaching, for He taught them as one having authority, and not as the scribes.

Matthew and Mark both testify almost word for word that Jesus taught with the wisdom and authority of God and not from man. The teachings of Christ had left His listeners with open mouths, but not always with open ears. The Scriptures tell us that they were astonished and impressed, but not always obedient as they listened to Him teach. His words are still alive with power and authority, yet we can see a world that is more impressed with the current headlines and the opinions of so-call experts, then in Christ. Nevertheless, the words of Christ can still have authority over every circumstance in our lives, if only we are willing to listen, believe and act on the eternal, faithful promises of God. His authority has not changed! He is still the Lord of lords and the King of all kings. His words still reflect His authority as any king or president would command an order. Jesus taught and still teaches with the authority of God.
Jesus taught with examples of nature and every day life. He speaks of the seed that falls to the ground, the farmer who tends the field, and the harvest that will come to those who have planted good or evil. He tells us about the rich man who is poor, because money is all that he has. He also tells us about the true riches of faith, where no thief can enter in and steal. He teaches us about love, peace and the value of faithfulness. He explains to us about the true bread, the living water and the fruit of the Spirit. He reassures us that though these bodies will fall apart and die, but the spirit is eternal. Most of all, Jesus teaches us about the ocean of God's love for us, and how that love should be a reflection toward one another. These words were and still are

astounding and should renew our spirits daily. Of course, we must read them on a consistent basis for them to take root in our hearts.

Mark 1: 21 & 13
Then they went into Capernanum and immediately on the Sabbath He (Jesus), *entered the synagogue and taught. Then He* (Jesus) *went out again by the sea; and all the multitude came to Him, and He taught them.*

Jesus taught in the temples, He taught on the mountains, He taught on the sea. Jesus taught His way to the cross, and even on the cross, He teaches us the greatest lesson of all. Of course, great signs of physical healing and spiritual deliverance followed His teaching, for what He taught happened in the hearts, bodies and minds of those who believed in His words.
One of my favorite lessons of the Master is when He illustrated how a true teacher should teach by example. The powerful lesson in this display of humility was simply to do as I say, and do as I do. Jesus holds nothing back in showing us the gentle, loving profile of God's care for us. In this case, Jesus gives us a lesson that we truly need to practice in our everyday life.

John 13: 5
After that, He (Jesus), *poured water into a basin and began to wash the disciple's feet, and to wipe them with a towel with which He was girded.*

Here we see something that as first will confuse our self-centered minds and leave us with our jaws scrapping the ground. The Master of all life, the King and Lord of all that exist, washes the dirtiest part of the disciple's bodies. Peter looked at Him and said to himself, 'Master, please do not do that!' Peter was confused as this lesson unfolded before his eyes. Here was deity in the suit of a man, but He was willing to become a servant and wash the feet of men. As Peter watches in shock, he responses in the way that most of the disciples wanted to, but were probably too dumbfounded to react. Peter, as usual jumps up to the plate, head first and expresses to Jesus exactly what is on his mind.

John 13: 6
Then He came to Simon Peter. And Peter said to Him, "Lord, are You washing my feet?"

Peter had witnessed the blind regain their sight, the deaf hear, the lame walk and the dead return to life. However, this lesson was more shocking then all of those put together. Peter waste no time in telling Jesus, 'No way will You wash my feet!'

John 13: 8
Peter said, "You shall never wash my feet."

Peter was beginning to understand that if your brother sins against you seventy times seven times, forgive him. He began to see the compassion toward the prostitute, the pickpocket tax collectors and the blind beggar who cried out for mercy. Peter was beginning to understand the tenderness of God, but this lesson left him in a state of resistance. Nevertheless, Jesus does wash his feet and gives them and us one of the most powerful lessons that He had ever taught.

John 1: 13 & 14
"You call Me Teacher and Lord and you do well, for so I am. If I then, your Lord and Teacher, have washed your feet, you also ought to wash one another's feet."

Jesus is certainly the Teacher of all teachers. This is one lesson that will puncture our pride and damage our egos. The only way we could learn from this example is to crucify our self-centered minds and truly live for the welfare of our sisters and brothers. Of course, Jesus was never self-centered; He was willing to give His all for the sake of saving us from an eternity of error. If we could only learn this lesson, we would be able to place our feet in the exact footprints where Jesus had stepped.

Psalms: 25 4, 5 & 8
Show me Your ways, O Lord; teach me Your paths, lead me in Your truth and teach me...
Good and upright is the Lord; Therefore, He teaches sinners in the way.

There is no doubt; we need to be taught by God. We have become so blind by the survivor viewpoint of the world that we forget that God is in control. Our faith becomes weak by the assaults of the enemy who uses people to manifest his evil presence in the natural. We need God's direction to correct the mental and spiritual wounds that have been sown in our minds and hearts for years. God knows that we need Him to teach us. Moreover, Jesus, who agreed to become our final blood sacrifice at the cross, agrees to teach us the principles of love, faith and mercy.

Mark 6: 2
And when the Sabbath had come, He (Jesus) *began to teach in the synagogue. And many hearing Him were astonished...*
"And what wisdom is this which is given to Him, that such mighty works are performed by His hands!"

What Jesus taught, He also performed. This is a clear picture that Jesus taught about God's power to heal and then displayed the power. Where there are teachings about the supernatural power of God to heal sickness, the manifestation of the power will be present. Jesus clearly illustrated the power of God through His teaching. However, in this particular instance, His hands were tied.

Mark 6: 1 & 5
Then He (Jesus) *went out of there and came to His own town...*
Now He could do no mighty works there, except that He laid His hands on a few sick people and healed them.

Can we tie the hands of God? Can we prevent God's blessings from reaching us? It is obvious that the people from the town where Jesus was raised as a Carpenter's Son were unwilling to except His teaching. Because of the rejection of His words, there were no mighty works done in that town. Jesus taught faith! Jesus sowed the word of God into the hearts of the listeners, but the believing part was their responsibility and our responsibility as well. You know the old saying, 'You can lead the horse to the water, but you can't make him drink.' God can lead us to a place of deliverance, a place of the pure living water of His word, but unless we drink of it, unless we believe, we will walk away empty. Do not be shocked that this could happen, without faith there is no hope. Jesus the Teacher taught this principle repeatedly throughout His earthly ministry.

Mark 5: 34
And He (Jesus), *said to her, "Daughter, your faith has made you well. Go in peace and be healed from your affliction."*

Jesus gives us illustration after illustration of how faith in Him will bring the manifest presence of God's supernatural power in to our bodies, our minds and our hearts if we only believe.
Some defined Jesus as a great preacher who captivated His listeners with poetic words of a better world through peace and love. However, Jesus is much more than that; He is the Teacher, the Master, and the Great Shepherd who laid His life down for His sheep. Jesus did preach the word of God to all that were willing to listen, but we need to define what accurate teaching really is. Some pastors preach for a reaction, a stirring up of the people as to bring them to a

place of enthusiasm. This might have some value in certain times or places, but Jesus preached by teaching faith, and faith will break through the walls of doubt that surrounds our lives. Jesus taught for change, not for a reaction. Jesus knows that when the word of faith is received in the spirit, it is like an explosion of power that will break through the strongholds of Satan and release the power of God.

Jesus was not some preacher who needed reassurance that what He was teaching was accurate. Jesus knew where He came from, Jesus knew what He was teaching and Jesus knew where He was going.

The Apostle Paul gives us a great insight of his own ministry in the manner of his teaching.

1st Corinthians 1:17 & 2:4
For Christ did not send me to preach (teach), the gospel, not with wisdom of words, lest the cross of Christ should be made of no effect.
And my speech and my preaching were not with persuasive words of human wisdom, but in demonstration of the Spirit and of power...

Paul did not need the reassurance or the approval of men. He knew where he had come from, (the kingdom of darkness), he knew what his assignment was, (teach and preach the gospel to the Gentiles), he knew where he was going, (with his Savior). He did not need to impress his listeners. Paul taught in the power of faith and then witnessed the results.

Jesus is not only the Author of our faith, but He is also the Finisher of our faith, and faith is nurtured by the teaching of the word of God. One of the greatest examples of how the disciples looked to Jesus to teach them how to operate in the principles of God was when they came to Him wanting to know how to pray. They consistently witnessed Jesus in prayer and any good student desires to be as their teacher, and so they asked.

Luke 11:1
Now it came to pass, as He was praying in a place, when He ceased, that one of His disciples said to Him, "Lord, teach us to pray, as John taught his disciples to pray."

The disciples were praying a pray and did not even realize it when they requested, *"Lord, teach us."* They looked to Jesus to be taught, and Jesus was glad to teach them.

Matthew 6:2, 6:34, 8:31, 4:1, 11:1
He began to teach them...
He began to teach them...
He began to teach them...
He began again to teach them...
He departed from there to teach and preach in their cities.

I believe that as much as Jesus loved to heal the sick, give sight to the blind, cleanse the leper and give hope to the hopeless, Jesus loved to teach during His earthly ministry. Jesus would sit down and teach one the same way he would teach a multitude of thousands. Moreover, when Jesus completed His mission, He promises another would come, a Teacher, a Holy Helper, who was sent not to condemn us, but to help us, to teach us and to guide us into eternity. It is obvious that God loves to teach us.

John 14: 26
"But the Helper, the Holy Spirit, whom the Father will send in My name, He will teach you all things..."

As the Holy Spirit is here to continue in teaching us all we need to know concerning the kingdom of God, listen to what Jesus commands us to do.

Matthew 28: 19 & 20
"Go therefore and make disciples of all nations, baptizing them in the name of the Father and of the Son and of the Holy Spirit, teaching them to observe all things that I have commanded you..."

The Teacher hands over the authority and responsibility to everyone who is taught; to every believer that has been redeemed by the grace. He commands us to go and do the same to someone else, as it had been done to us. Moreover, along with that command goes one of the greatest promises given to us by the Lord Jesus.

Matthew 28: 20
"I am with you always, even to the end of the age."

In a world that is full with uncertainty, and where evil can threaten our lives, our Lord and Teacher gives us a promise that will take us through this life and into eternity. He is a faithful Lord and Teacher, and teaches us the immeasurable value of being joined to Him, being a student, a disciple of His wonderful love. Moreover, as students we must also realize that no matter what our natural senses may indicate, God's word is the final authority in our every day situations. Jesus has never made a promise that He is unable to keep. As His beloved children, we are taught from a loving Father, our God who has already given us His heart and will continue as long as we are willing to receive it.

The High Priest

Hebrews 5:4
And no man takes this honor to himself, but he who is called by God, just as Aaron.

The Holy Spirit reveals to us the position of the high priest. Aaron, the brother of Moses was recorded in the Scriptures as one who was appointed by God for fulfilling the position of high priest. Although Aaron is not the first priest mentioned in the Scriptures, he is a good starting point to begin our search for the true meaning of the position. We first need to begin by reading the demand God placed on Moses. After God gave Moses the instructions for the structure of the tabernacle, the building of the mercy seat and the specific ornaments, He appoints Aaron as high priest and explains the job responsibilities.

Exodus 28:1 & 3
"Now Take Aaron your brother and his sons with him, from among the children of Israel that they may minister to Me as priest..."
"...That he may minister to Me as priest."

It is obvious that the original role given to Aaron as the high priest was to represent the children of Israel as a minister to God. What is a minister? A minister is someone who serves another, waits upon; attends to the needs or wants of another. Even a bondservant, who was not bound to stay in the service of his or her master, but willingly decided to serve rather than be free, were ministers to their masters. The Apostle Paul states that Apollos, Cephas (Peter), and himself were "ministers of Christ". As we read in the above text, Aaron's primary responsibility was to minister, serve, and attend to the wants of the Lord. We can say 'wants' because we know that God needs nothing, He is self-contained, all power, all knowing and all truth. However, it is obvious that God had a want, for if God did not have a want, we would not be here and neither would anyone else. God does not need us, but He wants us, He wants a relationship with us. Why does God want to have a relationship with us? I know many people think of themselves as an accident of birth, but the real reason why a person wants to bring a child into the world is to share their love with the child. A good parent has the seed of the love that God buried deep in their heart. They have a desire (a want), to share this love, unconditionally with no strings attached. Does God have a desire? There would be no other reason how to explain why God made man in *His image and likeness*. God wants to share His love with us in a relationship for eternity.

Now Aaron, as a representative, a bridge between God and the people, was to be a minister to the Lord as high priest, to give offerings of sacrifice to Him who called. This attempt to redeem himself and the people with the shedding of the blood of an innocent animal was a shadow of the things to come. Nevertheless, God shows the people of Israel, and us that sin is serious, so serious that even the attempt to cover it temporally could only be accomplish through the sacrifice of the innocent blood of an animal. The innocent for the guilty; a ransom, or a payment rendered. The high priest, as a servant of God who was called upon to offer the sacrifices, ministered to the Lord and represented the people as a mediator, a go between that stood in the gap between God and man. Man needed a high priest to present his sacrifice because of the separation between God and man caused by sin.

Hebrews 5:1
For every high priest taken from among men is appointed for men in the things pertaining to God, that he may offer both gifts and sacrifices for sins.

Beginning with Aaron and his sons, and on through the generations, the sacrifices were offered, year after year for the redemption of sins. We also see another priest, the first priest to be recorded in the book of Genesis.

Genesis 17:18
Then Melchizedek king of Salem brought out bread and
wine; he was a priest of God the Most High.

Where did this priest come from, or who ordained him a
priest? God gives us no history of this man and he was
never mentioned again in the book of Genesis. Some say
that this was Christ who meet with Abraham, as we do know
that God meet with Abraham on other occasions. Some
1000 years later, David writes a Psalm declaring Christ as a
priest.

Psalm 110:4
The Lord has sworn and will not relent, "You are a priest
forever according to the order of Melchizedek."

What is interesting about this oath is that Melchizedek is
referenced as a priest instead of Aaron who was appointed
in the first position of high priest. Christ was appointed High
Priest according to the order of someone we know little
about. We know Aaron's duties, as high priest was to
represent the people to God with a sacrifice for sin and to
minister to the Lord. What do we know about Melchizedek?
We know this priest blessed God, blessed Abraham and
brought out bread and wine. Bread and wine were common
with every meal, and was also offered in a covenant meal.
However, this meeting with Abraham was not just a meal,
this was a blessing, this was a holy moment in life of
Abraham, in that Abraham was so moved that he gave a
tenth of all he had to this priest. This was not just a religious
tradition, going through the motions of a service. Something
happened to the inner man of Abraham. Abraham's spirit
recognized the Spirit of God in this priest as he blessed
Abraham and in turn, Abraham gave to him. This
Melchizedek was divinely appointed, anointed by God as a
priest to serve the Most High with the sacrifice of praise, and
gave Abraham a blessing by the power of God. This priest
stood between God and man, offered praise and worship to

God, and blessing to man. Unlike the priesthood of Aaron, who represented man to God with a blood sacrifice, but not God to man with a blessing apart from the law.
Now Jesus entered humanity as the direct representative of God to man.

Philippians 2:6
…Who being in the form of God, did not consider it robbery to be equal with God, but made Himself of no reputation, taking the form of a bondservant, and coming to the likeness of men.

Jesus showed us the very nature of God, revealing God's merciful nature to His creation. Jesus taught, forgave, (which resulted in healing) and He comforted. Jesus then offered a one-time blood sacrifice for the atonement of sins for every man and woman. Not with the blood of bulls, goats or lambs, but He offered Himself as a final sacrifice. From this point on, He was now representing man to God as the High Priest. Who was now able to be a true representative for man, just as He was a true representative for God.

Hebrews 8:1
Now the main point of the things we are saying: We have such a High Priest, Who is seated at the right hand of the throne of the Majesty in the heavens, a Minister of the sanctuary and of the true tabernacle, which the Lord erected, and not man.

If Jesus had not become a man, He would not be able to represent us since He Himself would not have shared in our nature. This also works in the fact that Jesus represented God, since He Himself shared and still shares the very nature of God.

Hebrews 3:1
Therefore, holy brethren, partakers of the heavenly calling,
consider the Apostle and High Priest of our confession,
Christ Jesus.

What is the Holy Spirit asking us to consider? Consider the faithfulness of Jesus. He was faithful to God in representing the very nature of God to mankind, revealing God's heart toward us. He was also faithful in fulfilling all that was set before Him. Now this Jesus, who was faithful in representing God to us, is now also faithful as High Priest in representing us to God. As He had shared in the divine nature, representing God, He also shared in our human nature; therefore, He can be a true representative for us as our High Priest.

Hebrews 4:15
For we do not have a High Priest who cannot sympathize
with our weakness, but was in all points tempted as we are,
yet without sin.

Jesus can now be our true representative since He is one of us; just as He represented God, as He is also divine. Jesus is faithful in fulfilling the promises of God toward us, and fulfilling man's sacrifice to God for us as High Priest. Just as Jesus was faithful to the Godhead, to fulfill what God the Father had desired; He is also faithful to us, to represent us with a blood sacrifice for our sins.

Hebrews 7; 25
Therefore, He is also able to save to the uttermost those
who come to God through Him, since He always lives to
make intercession for them.

Anyone who comes to God through Jesus Christ are represented by Jesus Himself, who has every right to represent all those who believe in Him because He had paid the final sacrifice for sin with His own blood. No other sacrifice is needed, if we come to Him be faith. Therefore, it is faith in Him that fulfills the law. The innocent blood of a bull or a lamb is no longer required. For His sacrifice was so perfect, that we need only to believe in it and we are forgiven, cleansed from all our sins.

Hebrews 8:1
...We have such a High Priest, who is seated at the right hand of the throne of Majesty in the heavens.

We have a representative, One who speaks on our behalf, One that loves us with a passion in which words cannot describe. The very One that gave His life as an atonement for our sins. How much more will he bring our names before the throne of God in intercession on our behalf? This High Priest was able to represent God to us, being God; and now can represent us to God, being a Man. If Jesus was not both, He could not represent both. This is the true mystery of Christ, who entered the world as divine, but was and is a Man, now glorified and He sits at the right hand of the throne of God, a Man in the Godhead! Yes He is God, but He is also a Man, glorified as Faithful and True, the Lamb who was sacrificed for the redemption of all those who are willing to come to Him by faith.

Revelation 7:17
"For the Lamb (Jesus), *who is in the mist of the throne will shepherd them and lead them to living waters."*

The King

Psalm 24: 10
Who is the King of glory?

John 18:37
"You are a King then," said Pilate. Jesus answered, "You
are right in saying I am a King."

As Jesus is brought before the court of a Roman
commander, He stands charged before the most powerful
man around for miles, the direct representative to Caesar;
the high-ranking official named Pilate. If Pilate said you are
guilty, then your head is coming off. If Pilate judged you not
guilty, then you were free; no one dared to question Pilate.
They bring Jesus into this court and Pilate takes one look at
Jesus and thinks to himself, what threat does this man
possess? He has no weapon, no shield, no army, why is He
even in my court? Then Pilate begins to question Jesus as
He stands before the leader in silence, and this begins to
frustrate Pilate.

John 19:10
"Do you refuse to speak to me?" Pilate said. "Don't you
realize I have power either to free you or to crucify you?"

I can see Pilate pacing back and forth, shouting; 'don't you
know who I am? How can you disrespect me by not
answering my questions? Don't you know that I have
power?' I can see Pilate's face turning red and the veins
popping out of his neck. Pilate's anger begins to rage. Then
I can see Jesus raise His head and look Pilate in the eyes
and say;

John 19:11
"… You would have no power over Me if it were not given to
you from above."

What Jesus was really saying was, 'come down from your throne little man. If God did not have a purpose for you, then you would not have the position you now hold.' Then Jesus returns to His silence, unaffected by the shouts and rage of Pilate. Jesus knew who was in control.

This is not to say that the sufferings of Jesus were not real. He felt every sting of the whip, every blow to the head, every nail that split His skin open. However, Jesus knew the will of His Father.

Jesus breaks His silence when Pilate starts to rage in anger to reassure Pilate that everything is going as planned. It might have looked like Pilate, the Chief Priest, and all the other officials were in control, but this could not have been farther from the truth. It was not the people in control, but God.

When we can realize that God has a plan and is able to carry it out, then, we can also live our lives in faith and not in fear as Jesus clearly displayed for us, giving us an example to follow.

Now after Jesus said to Pilate that God is controlling these events, Pilate begins to back off.

John 19:12
From then on, Pilate tried to set Jesus free.

This is very interesting to see this man named Pilate, who just a minute ago was boasting about how much power he had, but now is powerless. Pilate tried to set Jesus free but could not. Pilate was the highest-ranking official for miles around, so what happened to all his power. All men are powerless when standing against the power of God.

So, we see the Man Jesus, standing in the middle of hate that you or I will never know. Here Jesus stands in silence. What was Jesus doing in that silence? If it were you or I, we would be demanding justice, we would be shouting for a fair trial. We would be asking God, God where are you now? Nevertheless, there stands the majestic Jesus; no threats, no hate, and no fear, Jesus knew that His heavenly Father was in complete control. Jesus stands with blood dripping from His head and pieces of skin hanging from His back. He stands in silence; He stands in faith and in the loving mercy of God the Father. Jesus stands before the butchers ready for the slaughter as a Man. We tend not to think about Jesus as a Man, but He was and is. Jesus felt every hit to the head, every lash of the whip, every insult and every lie against Him. The crowd who saw Him heal so many people, are all now gone. Jesus stands alone with a bloodthirsty crowd, looking for someone to die, and that someone was Him. I believe that Jesus had seen the cross from the very beginning, when Adam and Eve fell in the garden the cross was waiting for His blood.

As Jesus stands before Pilate, being judged from every side, He looks beyond the cross and beyond this world.

Revelation 4:2
Immediately I was in the spirit; and behold, a throne set in Heaven, and One sat on the throne.

Revelation 3:21
"To him who overcomes I will grant to sit with Me on My throne as I also overcame and sat down with My Father on His throne."

We can also look beyond our circumstances, beyond the troubled waters of these times and beyond the hurts and pains of this life. We can keep our eyes focused on the promise of God, because we know that God is faithful and true. If He promises us eternal life in His presence, then there should be no question that it is a reality for all that believe. We need to look beyond this temporary dwelling and focus on Him who promises us eternal life.

This Roman leader named Pilate was a politician and he could smell a railroading a mile away. Pilate knew the political arena; he was trained through experience on government affairs. Pilate saw right through this kangaroo court of Jews, with the trumped up charges that would have never stood up in a Roman court. Nevertheless, Pilate certainly was a politician, the kind that knows the right thing to do, but for fear of their political career, they decide to go along with the wrong. Let's take a ringside seat at the trial and begin to understand what Pilate began to see. As Pilate begins the inquiry, the first question he asked is; *"Are you a King?"* Pilate seems to be stuck on this question within him self. Pilate might have heard something about Jesus being a King, because he continually refers back to it.

John 18:33
The Pilate entered the Praetorium again, called Jesus, and said to Him, "Are You the King of the Jews?"

John 18:37
Pilate therefore said to Him, "Are you a King?"

John 18:39
"Do you want me to release the King of the Jews?"

John 19:14
"Behold your King."

John 19:15
Pilate said to them, "Shall I crucify your King?"

John 19:19
Now Pilate wrote a title and put it on the cross, and the writing was: JESUS OF NAZARETH, THE KING OF THE JEWS.

Pilate consistently refers to Jesus as *a King,* in that he even wrote the title of king and placed it on the cross of Jesus, and would not remove it.
Is Jesus the King of the Jews?

Psalm 10:16
The Lord is King forever and ever.
Let's look back to the days of Samuel when the people of
Israel had judges, including Samuel to rule over the day-to-
day affairs of the people. Samuel begins to age and the
people decided rather than have a prophet or a judge, they
wanted a king.

1st Samuel 8:6
*But the thing displeased Samuel when they said, "Give us a
king to judge us." So Samuel prayed to the Lord.*

Now Samuel knew that there was something wrong with this
request right from the start. Samuel listened to his spirit, and
his spirit was saying that this was a bad move.
Nevertheless, God hears and answers Samuel's prayer.

1st Samuel 8:7
*And the Lord said to Samuel, "Heed the voice of the people
in all that they say to you; for they have not rejected you, but
they have rejected Me, that I should reign over them."*

1st Samuel 12:12
...The Lord your God was your King.

Throughout the Old Testament, we read about the kings
who ruled over men. However, until this time there was no
king in the form of a man over the nation of Israel. God was
their King; He alone was their authority. We see God's
response to their request as He says, *"They have rejected
Me."* One of the things I find interesting about God is that
even as He was rejected, even as He knew that any man
would take advantage of the people as king, God was still
willing to fulfill their request. God was, and is still saying to
the people of every nation, that He will let us have what we
want, even if we decide to reject Him.

Nevertheless, God is the King of all and He alone should be our complete authority. Whatever choice we make does not change the truth. The people of Israel wanted a man for a king, and God desired to be their only King. Therefore, God became a Man and fulfilled their desires and His.

Now Pilate kept on asking Jesus, *"Are you a king?"* Pilate kept on referring to Jesus as the *King of the Jews*, even to the point that he wrote it on the cross and would not change what he wrote. God also refers to Himself as the *King of the Jews.*

Malachi 1:14
"For I am a great King," says the Lord of hosts, "And my name is to be feared among the nations.

Matthew 5:35
"...Nor by Jerusalem, for it is the city of the great King."

God states that He is the great King, and is calling Jerusalem the *city of the great King.* Therefore, God is the King of the Jews. This is what Pilate was calling Jesus, *the King of the Jews.* What was the response by Jesus when Pilate asked Him if He was the *King of the Jews?*

Matthew 27:11 Luke 23:3
Jesus said to him, "It is as you say it."

Pilate asked a straight foreword question and received a straight foreword answer. What were the people of Israel shouting when Jesus was healing their sick?

Luke 19:38
"Blessed is the King who comes in the name of the Lord!"

Jesus fulfilled the prophecy of Zechariah as He rides on a humble donkey into the city of Jerusalem.

Zachariah 9:9
Behold, your King is coming to you: He is just and having
salvation, lowly and riding on a donkey...

God states clearly that He is the King of His chosen and
Jerusalem is His City. Jesus confesses to be the *King of the*
Jews, the King of the city and the King who rules and reigns
over the hearts of all those who are willing to receive Him as
Lord, Savior and King.

Isaiah 42:15
"I am the Lord, your Holy One, The Creator of Israel, your
King."

The Israelites, did not need a man for a king, they had God.
"I am the Lord...Your King." Nevertheless, they received
both. Jesus fulfilled every prophecy concerning the Savior,
the Christ and the King who was, who is and who is to come
again. Jesus is the *King of Jews!*

1st Timothy 6:13
I urge you in the sight of God who gives life to all things, and
before Christ Jesus who witnessed the good confession
before Pontius Pilate...

What was the good confession of Jesus before Pilate?
Remember the question that Pilate asked Jesus repeatedly.
Remember how Pilate kept referring to Jesus as the *King of*
the Jews.

1st Timothy 6:15
...He (God), *who is the blessed and only Sovereign, the*
King of kings and the Lord of lords who alone has
immortality, dwelling in the unapproachable light, whom no
man has ever seen or can see, to whom be honor and
everlasting power.

Revelation 17:14
…*"And the Lamb* (Jesus), *will overcome them, for He*
(Jesus), *is the Lord of lords and the King of kings, and those*
who are with Him (Jesus)*, are called, chosen, and faithful."*

Revelation 19:16
And He (Jesus) *has on His robe and on His thigh a name*
written: KING OF KINGS AND LORD OF LORDS.

God revealed to Samuel, Isaiah, Malachi and David that He
is the eternal *King of kings* who rules the heavens and earth.
Even the King Nebuchadnezzar, prophesized that the God
of Daniel was *Lord of all kings.* Though Pilate was blind to
God's plan as he gave Jesus the final judgment of death, he
recognized Jesus as the *King of the Jews.*
Jesus Christ, who sits in the unapproachable light of God
(the Godhead); which no mortal man has ever or could ever
see in His full manifestation, is the King. He is the King of
the Jews, the King of the earth, the King of all nations, the
King of the heavens, the King of men's hearts, the King of all
kings, the King of all! Every king has a kingdom, and His
kingdom shall see no end. His kingdom will last beyond the
limitations of time, beyond the natural and into the
supernatural, which is beyond our current comprehension.

Daniel 2:44
"And in the days of these kings, the God of Heaven will set
up a kingdom which shall never be destroyed; and the
kingdom shall not be left to other people; it shall break in
pieces and consume all these kingdoms, and it shall stand
forever."

God has set His kingdom in place and Jesus Christ will
return to gather the citizens of the eternal inheritance. Jesus
will come again with many crowns of glory on His head as
King and Lord.

Psalm 47: 2, 6, & 7
For the Lord Most High is awesome; He is a great King over
all the earth.
Sing praises to God, sing praises!
Sing praises to our King, sing praises!
For God is the King of all the earth;
Sing praises with understanding.

The Scriptures clearly define God as the *King of the earth,*
He is the *Lord Most High*, the final authority, and we can
rejoice and sing praises for that fact.

Zachariah 9:9
Rejoice greatly. O daughter of Zion! Shout O daughter of
Jerusalem! Behold, your King is coming to you; He is just
and having salvation...

The prophet Zechariah sees the King of kings from a
distance as he reassures the people of Israel that the King is
coming. Israel was told that a day was coming when the
King of all the earth would ride in to Jerusalem on a humble
colt as a living sacrifice, the Savior of all who believe.
However, the Apostle John also sees the King coming
again.

Revelation 19:11 & 16
Now, I saw the heavens opened, and behold, a white horse.
And He (Jesus), *who sat on him...*
And He (Jesus) *has on His robe and on His thigh a name*
written: KING OF ALL KINGS AND LORD OF ALL LORDS.

Psalm 10: 16
The Lord is the King forever and ever.

The Scriptures tell us about three wise men that received a
revelation about the birth of a Child. As the three wise men
approach Jerusalem, they give the answer to the question

that Pilate had asked the Lord Jesus repeatedly some thirty years later, as the King stands before the Roman court.

Matthew 2:1, 2
Behold, wise men came from the East to Jerusalem, saying, "Where is He who has been born the King of the Jews?

The Light

John: 7: 9
This man came for a witness, to bear witness of the light
that through him all might believe. He was not the Light, but
was sent to bear witness of that Light. That was the true
Light, which gives light to every man coming into the world.

John's true mission, to be a witness of the Light. He was not
sent to be a witness for any other purpose. He was not
called to be a witness to the Law of Moses, or to be a
witness to the rituals of the Jewish customs. The calling in
which he was sent was to bear witness of the Light, the true
Light that came into the world and gives light to every man.
Who is the true Light?

John 1: 10
He was in the world, and the world was made through Him,
and the world did not know Him.

This Light, by whom the world was made though, was not
known by the world, because the world was, and still is in
the darkness of sin. It is hard to see anything in the dark.
It is interesting how many times in Scripture that God refers
to darkness as a lack of knowledge, the absence of
revelation light that shines on those who are willing to trust
the Creator at His word. Darkness is the lack of the light of
understanding in the heart of men. John the Baptist clearly
received a true revelation on the identity of the Light that
reveals the knowledge of God.

Psalm 27: 1
The Lord is my light and my salvation; whom shall I fear?

The psalmist declares that God is his Light, and as long as
we follow and focus on the Light, we have no one to fear.
The Apostle John also gives us a declaration of faith in the

deity of Jesus Christ as the Light that shines in the darkened hearts of men.

1st John 1: 5
God is light and in Him there is no darkness.
John 1: 9
That was the true Light, which gives light to every man coming into the world.

There is a Light; some may call it a conscience, some might call it the inner voice of God. This Light is present and can be manifested within us if we have discovered it with an open heart in surrender to Christ. As the sun gives forth light throughout the orbiting planets that surround it, so the Son gives light into the spirits of men and women. Whether we make a choice to drown this light with the darkness of sin, or abide in the light with the flame of faith, the Light is still present. The true Light is life, for life is of the spirit. Moreover, Jesus is declared as the Giver of light and the true Light which came into the natural.

John 1:4
In Him (Jesus), *was life, and the life was the light of men.*

Therefore, the light of men is the very spark of life that ignites each heartbeat that sends our blood rushing through our bodies. The light is the life within us; it is in our spirits that contain the power of existence in the natural and the supernatural for eternity. As the sun is the source of light for the natural, Jesus is the Light, the source of life by the supernatural power of God that fills these natural bodies with God's gift of life!

John 8:12
Then Jesus spoke to them again, saying, "I am the light of the world. He who follows Me shall not walk in darkness, but have the light of life."

Revelation 21:23
The city had no more need of the sun or of the moon to shine in it, for the glory of God illuminated it. The Lamb is its light.

The Apostle John paints a picture of the majesty of God as he witnessed the glory of Jesus Christ, as God illuminates the heavens with the pure light of life. *The Lamb,* Jesus Christ is the Light in our hearts and in all of heaven, and He gives life to all that believe in His name, to the glory of God the Father, forever!

The Enemy of the King

Isaiah 14: 12
"How you have fallen from heaven O Lucifer, son of the
morning!

The prophet Isaiah had received a powerful revelation on
the fall of an enemy of God, and now an enemy of us. Does
God really have an enemy? Satan is the true enemy of
Jesus Christ and His church. Does this enemy have power
over man? He has no power over us, only the power that we
give him over our lives. God tells us that there is a fallen
angel, a rebel whose heart became filled with pride.
Moreover, that sin led him into a dark, lost, perverted
thought pattern that is still torturing his spirit. He is a
defeated foe. Nevertheless, he is still an active enemy of
Jesus Christ, and will deceive many people who are willing
to believe his lies. Is a fallen, defeated angel worthy to be
mentioned in a book that gives praise, honor and glory to
our Lord and Savoir? It is not a question of Satan being
worthy to be noted, but rather it is for our benefit that we
comprehend the rebellion this fallen being has against our
God and our position on the front lines. Furthermore, the
enemy has gathered together troops that are ready and
willing to destroy us since they are unable to reach God.
The saddest part of this war is that this enemy hates the
civilian (the unbeliever), just as much as he hates the soldier
(the believer), just as much as he hates the King (God
Almighty).

Ephesians 6:12
For we do not wrestle against flesh and blood, but against
principalities, against powers, against the rulers of the
darkness of the age.

So, who are the unseen enemy forces that wage war
against God and us? The above Scripture gives us some
great insight on what we are dealing with in spiritual warfare.

Let us establish some facts given to us in the timeless word of God. The enemies that attempt to invade our lives are not flesh and blood. It is not the drunk or the dope addict, the thief, the rapist, or the murderer who drinks the blood of his victims. They are all flesh and blood. It is not the person on the job that will lie, cheat and play politics to gain favor from the boss. It is not the guy, who beats his wife and abuses his children; they are flesh and blood. It is not the guy who sold you that used car, who forgot to tell you all the things wrong with it; he is flesh and blood. So who are these enemies? They are spiritual, unseen beings, fallen angels who have turned against God and follow their leader, Satan. Sounds like some kind of science fiction movie? These rulers of darkness are as real as the person that is standing next to you.

It started with a rebellious angel named Lucifer. Here are some undisputed facts about Satan and his army of demons. They are spirits, not flesh and blood. They rule over darkness, the wicked and sin infested hearts. They enter in and take charge over the minds and hearts of those without understanding. These rebellious, seducing spirits will use people so they can destroy the lives of many that become victims of their hate. Satan knows that by hurting us, it also hurts God, and this is the main objective in this war.

Still sounds like some far out science fiction movie? Guess again! There is no doubt that these evil spirits not only exist, but also are engaged in an active war against God and all that believe in the Lord Jesus Christ, the King.

Another very important fact is that these evil spirits can enter into a person, if they are allowed, and attempt to torture the victim with mental illness, sickness, diseases and crimes against God and humanity. Again, their war is against God, and humanity is used as a vessel by which they will attack repeatedly to achieve their objective.

In the Gospel of *Matthew 17:18, 8:16, 8:31 and 32,* and *Luke 9:1,* we see the Lord Jesus casting these spirits out of

the residence of people. They were in children, at times in adults, but they were in people.
Still sounds like some Hollywood movie? Read God's word; there is no mistake about these evil spirits! Peter had received a revelation about the leader of these evil spirits.

1st Peter 5:8 and 9
Be self-controlled and alert, your enemy the devil prowls around like a roaring lion looking for someone to devour.

Let's take a good look at this revelation from God about the enemy. If you or I decided to go hiking in the woods somewhere in the mountains, in a very desolate area and someone gives us a clear warning to beware, would we listen? They warn us to be alert, stay sober, because there are grizzly bears in these woods, and if they catch you, they will tear you to pieces! Well, we might not decide to go hiking in that area, but if we did decide to go in those woods, our minds would be looking for any creature that even looked like a bear. I do not think we would just walk through those woods as though there were no dangers. We would be on the alert and aware of every branch that moved. It would also be a very good idea to bring a weapon, just in case one of those huge animals decided to show up and have you for lunch.
God, through the Apostle Peter, gives us the same type of warning. Be on your guard, be alert; watch out for signs of his presence, because he is looking for someone to devour and it could be one of us! If we can know the signs of his attack, then we can be one the alert.

Ephesians 4:27
Neither give place to the devil.

1st Peter 5:9
Resist him, standing firm in the faith.

James 4:7
Resist the devil, and he will flee from you.

What did God tell the Apostles, Paul, Peter and James? Let me use another illustration to show the battle plan of the enemy. He is trying to convince us that God is not really who He says He is and that God does not care for us. He does not want anyone to come to the knowledge of God's love in Jesus Christ. Once someone does discover the truth of God, the enemy is fighting a losing battle, because the only weapon he has is a lie! Look at how he convinced Adam and Eve to disobey God by eating the forbidden fruit. That disobedient action, sin, caused the human race to fall under the curse of the devil.

If you are someone who smokes cigarettes and the doctor tells you to stop or it will damage your health, do you listen? Then someone else, whether a friend or not comes up to you and says, 'cigarettes never hurt anybody,' who are you going to believe? This is a good example because people ignore the warnings about their physical health as well as their spiritual salvation. If we ignore the warnings about our spiritual health, then we are in a danger zone, just as if we ignore the warnings about our physical health.

Some might say that if this is true, then what defense or offense do we have against these enemies? There are two heavy weapons at the believer's disposal against the bloodthirsty acts of the devil and his troops. When Jesus won the war as a sacrifice on the cross for our sins, died and rose on the third day, Satan and his army were stripped of all their authority. They now only have the authority over us if we choose to surrender it to them. Remember, the battle is against God, but whether we believe it or not, we are all stationed on the battlefield. An unbeliever is like a civilian in the center of the battlefield, with no weapons, no supplies and no general to lead them to victory. On the other hand, a born again, bible reading, prayer devoted believer has the spiritual weapons of God at his or her disposal. Whether the soldier (the believer), chooses to use these weapons or not, will determine the defeat or victory in his or her life.

In the sixth chapter of the Epistle to the Ephesians we receive a hand-to-hand combat guide against the devil and his demons using the armor of God in which Jesus paid for with His own blood.

The most offensive weapon named here is *"The Sword of the Spirit, which is the Word of God."* The same word that Jesus used to defeat Satan when tempted can still be used to slice every demonic force in to ribbons! When the enemy attempts to inject dark, evil thoughts into our minds, we now know that we are engaged in spiritual warfare. How else can Satan and his followers attempt to lure us away from God and into bondage? We are prisoners of war if we allow hate, anger and unbelief to overcome us. If we abuse our bodies, abuse our lives into the captivity of sin, we are then slaves to the very things that can and will destroy us?

Again, this is not a game, a movie, or someone's imagination trying to sell a book. The devil and his demons are real. Moreover, to effectively stop them, we need to follow God's instructions very closely as a soldier would follow the command of a general, or we will suffer and be a prisoner of torment by demonic forces.

The devil is looking to control our lives by controlling our thought patterns for the use of destroying us and hurting God. Many people never realize that they have submitted their will, their thoughts to an evil spirit who wants nothing less then to kill them and use them to destroy other people. How else can a being control another being unless first he captures their thoughts and convinces them to think the way he thinks?

Once a thought pattern is fully developed, then the actions of those thoughts are soon to follow. Any leader of any army in history has been able to control his forces by controlling the thinking of his troops. Unlike a general of an army who is seeking the victory for his troops, the devil is seeking destruction for anyone who is willing and blind enough in submitting to his evil desires. Seducing thoughts that are sin will certainly lead to spiritual death!

The key to unlocking the door of our wills is to control our thoughts. If the enemy can convince us that God does not care, that God is the enemy and that God does not forgive us, then we have no hope. If he can convince us that Jesus is not who He says He is, then we are open targets with a bull's eye on our back and with no weapon of faith.

Remember the word of the Lord that Peter received, *"Be self-controlled and alert."* We cannot sleepwalk through this life thinking the battle is for someone else to fight. When the enemy comes knocking on our door, we will be defenseless unless we know how to fight back by the word and power of God. The devil is a deceiver, a liar that practices the art of deception. He is not going to just blow his cover by showing us some demonic manifestation of his existence. If anything, he wants us to believe that he does not exist at all, and the thoughts that are attempted to be injected in our minds are our own.

Now, the totally spiritless person is going to read this and say, your crazy, nuts, gone off the deep end, because he or she has no spiritual insight in the word of God. They are blind to the thoughts of God, so it will seem as rubbish, foolish talk, words from a far out imagination. They are being deceived in such a subtle way, that they do not even realize the battle that is going on around them. It is like getting your wallet picked from your pocket. You do not have a clue what is happening when the well-trained pickpocket gently separates you from your wallet. The devil will gentle separate us from God until we have drifted so far away that we have lost our way back. Then, at the point of hopelessness, he will attempt a fatal blow, and there we stand, defenseless, unable to fight, with our back to the wall. Even in that state, if we drifted so far away from God that all life seems hopeless, there is a still a way. There still is the most powerful weapon, the bomb of all bombs. This missile will cause every demon from hell, including Satan, to run with their tail between their legs, trying to get out of the way as fast as they can. This powerful, super weapon will cause them to tremble, flee in fear; and that weapon is the name of the Lord Jesus Christ that is used in faith. When we call out to God in the name of Jesus, combined with faith, every demonic spirit is going to start running as far away from you as they can get! When the Holy Spirit comes on the scene in the power of the name of Jesus Christ, by the power of God the Father, look out demons!

James 2:19
You believe that there is one God. You do well. Even the demons believe and tremble!
Luke 8:28
When he,(a demon) saw Jesus, he cried out, fell down before Him and with a loud voice said, "What have I to do with You, Jesus Son of the Most High God? I beg you. Do not torment me!"

Throughout the gospels we read how these demonic spirits tremble with fear at the presence of Jesus. When the Apostle James wrote the words, *they tremble,* he saw it first hand. God is all mighty, no devil or demon can stand in the power of His presence, they all have to flee or bow. The Apostle Peter and the Apostle James both witnessed the power of God through Jesus Christ. Matthew, a record keeper by profession, records Jesus casting out demonic spirits who had taken a person in the bondage of sickness. Matthew was called to record the things he had witnessed with his own eyes.

Matthew 17:18, 8:16, 8:31 and 32
...The demon and it came out of the boy...
...And He cast out spirits with His word, and healed all that were sick.
And when they came out, they went into a herd of swine.

We read about demonic spirits being ordered to leave a person's body by our Lord and Savior Jesus Christ. Did

Matthew, Peter and James see the demonic spirit leave the person? These spirits are not visible through the natural eye. Jesus spoke to these evil spirits, casting them out as they trembled with fear. In every case, the ones who were held prisoner by evil were set free, healed, cured, and glorified God after being released from the bondage of evil. Still think that all this stuff about the devil and demonic spirits are just in Hollywood? That is exactly what they want us to believe. After all, why have weapons for someone who does not exist? God says He has an enemy and so do we! His name is Satan and he leads a pack of fallen angels called demons. If we refuse to understand that there is a war over our souls all around us, then we are calling God a liar. Know that God is all truth, all light, and in Him there is no darkness.

2nd Peter 2:4
For God did not spare the angels who sinned, but cast them down to Hell and delivered them into chains of darkness to be reserved for judgment.

God makes this very clear that fallen angels have been cast into the darkness of evil and will be judged.

Luke 10:18 and 19
He replied, "I saw Satan fall like lightening from Heaven. I have given you authority to trample on snakes and scorpions and to overcome all the power of the enemy; nothing will harm you.

You really think that there is no Satan, no fallen angels, or no enemy to overcome? God says there is! This enemy is already defeated, stripped of all his power. Jesus Christ has already crushed his head!

Jude 1:6
And the angels who did not keep their positions of authority, but abandoned their own home, these He has kept in

darkness, bound with everlasting chains for judgment on that great day.

Again, we see the cursed fallen angels, thrown into blindness, the darkness of evil, chained with the weight of sin, and being held for judgment. There should be no doubt in our minds that these fallen angels have been polluted by their own sin, which has caused a transformation from good to evil. They are prisoners of their own darkness, trapped in the dark, gloomy dungeons of their disobedience to God and have convinced many to follow them. No grace, no mercy, or no hope has been given to these beings. They have clearly made a choice to follow the dark evil of Satan and have turned away from the loving light of God. Without any hope by grace, the only thing that awaits them is judgment. God did not spare them. Why is there no grace for them, and mercy for us? Maybe because they beheld the Glory of God, living in the very presence of His full manifestation. There was no faith required; yet, they still turned away from the living God to follow a created being named Satan. There will never be any mercy for these beings, only judgment. Where faith is required, then there is grace. God's mercies are poured out on the one who is willing to trust Him by faith. Through the blood of Jesus Christ, we have obtained God given faith that gives birth to eternal salvation. All because of the sacrifice of Jesus Christ, in Him we have all the riches of God, and are set free from the chains of sin, no longer prisoners of war.

2nd Peter 1:1
To those who have received like precious faith with us by the righteousness of our God and Savior Jesus Christ.

Peter refers to our *God and Savoir, Jesus Christ.* Peter is speaking about God the Son who is the Author of our faith and *the Author of our salvation.* It is through faith in Him that we have been redeemed, set free and fully equipped to resist our enemy when he attempts to take ground in our lives. No fallen angel can claim this faith; they all know that they are doomed for eternity! Why waste our time reading about these fallen beings? Why even waste one minute in writing these notes? God says:

"Be sober; be vigilant; because your adversary the devil walks about..."

God is saying to all of us to be aware and know that we have an enemy. No soldier, when in an enemy territory will just walk around without any awareness that there is an enemy. A good soldier is always watching when on enemy grounds. His eyes are looking for anything uncommon, his ears are listening for unusual sounds and his weapon is always ready to be used. We are indeed on enemy grounds since the Scriptures calls Satan *the prince of the air.* Most of us think that we have nothing to be concerned about; we know right from wrong and good from evil, so we can recognize the darkness of evil. Do not be so over confidant in your own abilities. After all, if not for the Holy Spirit in us, directing us, we would be sitting ducks, open season for Satan and his followers. God says, *"Be sober."* He is not talking about not having cocktails after dinner. He is telling us to watch out, be on our guard, for our enemy is seeking someone to destroy, and that someone is you and I. If you have been saved by the blood of Jesus Christ, sealed in the Holy Spirit, born in the family of God, then God is your Father and He knows how to take care of all of His children who have placed their trust in Him. If you have not been born into the family of God through faith in Jesus Christ, you are an open, unprotected target for the enemy. Remember that God is still giving us a warning to be careful. For while we are under God's protection, His arm wrapped around us, we still have the free choice to turn left or right. Holy angels are around us, the Holy Spirit is inside us, and we are in God's care, but we still have decisions to make everyday. The goal and objective of the enemy is to slowly pull us out of God's protection by making ungodly choices.

He will try to cause us to drift away from God little by little, and before we realize it, we begin to depend on our own strength instead of God's power. Once we have drifted so far away from God that we begin to think we can handle our own lives, spiritually and naturally, the enemy is close. He has us in full view as a hunter who finally has a chance at his prey. When that happens, we can classify these conditions as drunk by the flesh. Not drunk by some alcohol beverage, but drunk by pride and selfishness, thinking that we are saved, therefore, we have nothing to be concerned about. In some cases, we think that we are saved by our own self-righteousness. Once this thinking pattern begins, then the enemy already has us in a stronghold, a spiritual headlock. Little by little, he will begin to apply more and more pressure, attempting to choke out the very life that is within us. Ever so slowly, he will squeeze us, tighter and tighter, offering his solutions to relieve the pressure. He will not apply too much, too fast, knowing that too much pain will cause us to go running back to God in repentance. He is willing to go slow, so slow that we will not realize what is going on until we find ourselves in a panic, full of fear and empty on faith.

The enemy has been doing this for six thousand years. Could you imagine if an artist was painting for thousands of years, what his paintings would look like? Can you imagine if any one of us had six thousand years to practice his or her craft or hobby and how well we would know it? Imagine the musician who could have practiced for thousands of years. The devil and his demons have had thousands of years and many practice victims to work on their craft.

So, God says, *"Be sober."* If we are not moved by the deception of the enemy, if we are sober, aware of his motives, if we stand on the word of God and not in our own strength, he will flee from us. Our weapon is the word of God, and the sober soldier keeps his weapon cleaned, loaded and ready to fire at any given time. The enemy has no chance against the armed soldier. Our weapon is the living word of God, and Jesus Christ is the Word and has already defeated the enemy. Do not allow your weapon to become full of dust, unloaded and forgotten, sitting on a bookcase. Our weapon, the word of God needs to be loaded daily in our hearts and minds, stored and ready to be used at any time the enemy draws fire. Nothing will work faster to cause the enemy to run except the word of God used in faith, in the name of Jesus Christ. Our own strength, our willpower, our reasoning, our self-esteem will fail when it comes to over taking the deceitfulness of Satan. When we use the most powerful weapon given to us by God, the enemy is helpless and wounded with no other choice, but to leave.

Galatians 6:3
For if anyone thinks himself to be something, when he is nothing, he deceives himself.

Do not attempt to fight these demonic fallen angels in your own power. You will fail! It was not by your own power that you came to the throne of grace, but by the power of the word of God.

Ephesians 6:17, Hebrews 4:12
...The sword of the spirit, which is the word of God...

For the word of God is living and powerful, and sharper than any two-edged sword...

If we stand on the word of God, the enemy will continue to be defeated in our lives. Men and women throughout the history of humanity have fallen to the deception of Satan, like Adam through Judas, and on and on. Out of selfishness, gluttony, jealousy, pride, greed, unforgiving, a lust for power, and with the attitude of rebellion against the word of God, men and women have fell deep in the darkness of error.

Ephesians 4:27
Neither give place to the devil.

Does this mean that the true believer will live like a monk in a monastery somewhere in the mountains? No! Does it mean that a true believer will live on the constant edge of paranoia, looking, waiting for when the enemy might strike? No! God is telling us to simply, *"Be sober,"* be aware that there is an enemy and beware of his lures of deception. Do not be like the ostrich that sticks his head in a hole when there is danger, thinking he is safe and protected, just because he does not see the danger. God gave us a weapon to fight back by the power of His word, the very word that called all things into existence. What could be more powerful than that? Whether we decide to use it is up to us, it is our choice. However, it is there for us to live in victory. Therefore, when we go through an attack of the enemy, and it seems like there is no way out, our backs are against the wall, listen to what God tells us to do!

Ephesians 6:16 and 17
...Taking the shield of faith... ...Take the helmet of salvation ...And the sword of the Spirit, which is the word of God.

Take the armor and weapon of God, suit up and trust God, because the power of God is available to every believer. The enemy knows that against the power of God, the sword of the Spirit, he will fall and retreat from his attack every time we use the word of God against him in faith.
When Satan tempted Jesus, he first approached Him by challenging His flesh with the thought of food. Jesus answered, *"It is written..."* Again, the devil attempts to appeal to His flesh by saying, 'I will give you the world.' Again, Jesus answered, *"It is written."* However, something very strange happened the third time that Satan approaches Jesus. Satan says, *"It is written."*
Now let us just follow this pattern and gain some insight on what was Satan's battle plan? He attempts to win the Man

Jesus through His immediate needs, food for His flesh. Does Satan tempt us with the needs for our flesh? Did not he tempt Adam and Eve in the same manner? Satan will appeal to our fleshly appetites and the desires of our natural minds. Therefore, Satan's first allurement will be to bait us with the desires and needs of the flesh, our naturalism. When we can say to him, *it is written, man shall not live by bread alone, but by every word of God,* then, he begins to play on our greed, our thirst for power, our pride and our wanting to be someone important. In the second temptation of Satan to Jesus, Satan reveals to us what he really is looking for. He wants to be worshipped as a god. Can you imagine; not only a created being, but also a fallen angel who wants to be worshipped! So Jesus picks up the sword of the Spirit again and says, *"It is written. You shall worship the Lord your God and Him only you shall serve."* At this point, appealing to the natural desires that had worked for so many others in history, fails against Jesus. So, Satan gives it one last pitch and said to Jesus, *"It is written."* He attempts to distort the word of God by twisting the meaning so it is void, like an unloaded gun, instead of the perfect weapon that it is.

We ask ourselves, why are there so many different churches and doctrines? Why are there so many different interpretations of the same word? Why do some believe some parts of the word of God and disregard with others? I believe the answer is in this chapter of the Gospel of Luke. When all else fails, Satan goes along with giving people a distorted, twisted view of God's word. You can see why the Apostles John, Peter, Paul and James received a clear warning from God about false teachers. Satan will attempt to lead us in error, even if it is a matter of distorting the word of God, making the word void with no effect. Therefore, when Satan tested Jesus by a misinterpretation of the word of God, Jesus comes right back at him with the true Scripture. Therefore, the devil, who has no authority except for what we give him, will try three basic baits.

The first, he appeals to the needs of our natural life. The thought pattern, that as long as we are full and warm, everything is just fine, like keeping an infant content.
The second is to appeal to our pride and our thirst to be on top, the boss, the leader; our carnal way of thinking.
When all else fails, he gives us a religion that is in error. In other words, as long as we do not know that God has provided a sword to cut into the devil and his demons, we cannot use it.

Therefore, these empty religions are no threat to him. They misinterpret the word of God, leaving the members as an open target for the devil's hunt. Make no mistake in thinking that the temptations of the devil are a test, they are not a test, they are attacks! Satan will try to bring us to a place where we have lost our armor of protection, our faith and our knowing what the word of God says and how to use it.
When evil begins to break out around you, it is not a test; it is another attack in an ongoing war. Now out of these attacks, we will become stronger, knowing that the mighty power of God's word will work for our victory over the assault of these demonic spirits, if we stand fast on the promises of God in faith. If we do not, if we lose our faith, this is not just a test, this is not a game, and the enemy will then begin to come in *to steal and destroy*. Once we are unprotected by losing the shield of faith and dropping the sword of the Spirit, the enemy is going to just walk right in.

Mark 3:27
No one can enter a strong man's house and plunder his goods, unless he first binds the strong man. And then he will plunder his house.
This Scripture has a double meaning. Both have to do with the battle against evil forces. We can either bind Satan or be bound by him with false teachings.
2nd Corinthians 11:14 and 15
And no wonder! For Satan himself transforms himself into an angel of light. Therefore, it is no great thing if his

ministers also transform themselves into ministers of righteousness.

When Satan attempts to invade our lives, our work, our home, even our church, it is an attack. If we stand on the word of God, not shaken or moved by what we see, then our foot is against the devil's neck. If we are moved by our circumstances, the devil's foot is against ours. Remember this is not a test. Satan's main and foremost objective is to stop the knowledge of Jesus Christ, because he knows that he must flee when the name of Jesus is used in faith. He also knows that it is faith in the name of Jesus Christ that will redeem the sinner, and will give eternal life to those who have been imprisoned in his cell of death. Jesus Christ, and all those who believe in His name has an enemy, but he is a defeated enemy, stripped of all authority. Nevertheless, he will continue to attack the lives of every believer, and will continue to fail if we keep the faith in Jesus Christ.

"And His name (Jesus Christ), *through faith in His name, has made this man strong. ...Given him this perfect soundness in the presence of you all." Acts 3:25*

Our Rescuer

Ezekiel. 34.12
As a shepherd seeks out his flock when some of his sheep
have been scattered abroad, so I will seek out My sheep;
and I will rescue them from all places where they have been
scattered on a day of clouds and thick darkness.

The only survivor of a shipwreck was washed up on a small,
uninhabited island. He prayed feverishly for God to rescue
him. Exhausted and beginning to lose hope, he managed to
build himself a little hut out of driftwood to protect him from
the elements, and to store his few possessions.
Then one day, after scavenging for food, he arrived at his
home base to find his little hut in flames, and the smoke
rolling up to the sky. He became angry and sorrowful and
cried out to God, "How could you do this to me?" Everything
that he had was gone and he could not understand how God
could let this happen.
Early the next day, he was awakened by the sound of a
ship. The men from the ship screamed, "We are here to
rescue you." "How did you know I was here?" asked the
weary man of his rescuers. They replied, "We saw your
smoke signal."
There are times in our lives when we are unable to
understand why we have lost something or why everything
we worked for has just gone up in smoke. We need to
remember that God is working and He is our Rescuer.
Though we might not understand His methods, we know
that the outcome is for our good. Even in the thick clouds of
trouble and the dark nights of sorrow, God is our Great
Shepherd who will protect and direct His flock out of His
merciful love. When we were shipwrecked on an Island of
rebellion, God sent a Vessel of Redemption on a rescue
mission to save what was lost.

Romans 5:8
But God demonstrates His love toward us, in that while we
were still sinners, Christ died for us

The above text defines a divine rescue mission in that man was unable to rescue himself, drowning in his own sin. Unable to defeat the massive waters of evil, so you and I were caught in the tide of darkness, disillusioned by the enemies' lies. Then the Rescuer came. For when someone is drowning in the sea of their own sin, they are unable to rescue themselves. A natural drowning man cannot swim to safety; that is why he is drowning, overtaken by the force of the waters.

Revelation 19: 11
Now I saw heaven open, and behold, a white horse. And He who sat on him was called Faithful and True, and in righteousness He judges and makes war.

Jesus will return one day riding in on a white horse with all power and glory for a final battle against evil. However, two thousand years ago, the Lord Jesus rode in on a humble donkey, captured the bad guys, but then broke the chains of deception and death. He took back the stolen treasure of life that Adam had so carelessly given to the murderer (Satan), and made a public spectacle of the evil outlaws of heaven. He did it while we were held prisoners in a camp of darkness, helpless and unable to see the light of hope. Jesus, the King and Lord of all life took on the bad guys and won! Through His death, we have forgiveness; through His resurrection, we have eternal life.

Acts 3: 14: 15
"But you denied the Holy One and the Just, and asked for a murderer to be granted to you, and killed the Prince of Life. Whom God raised from the dead, of which we are witnesses."

Do you think that there is another way into the mercy of God's grace? Think again! The cost for this rescue mission was immeasurable, yet it was paid in full. God looked for a man to fulfill the mission, but could not find one who was not a prisoner himself. Therefore, God sent someone who is a direct representative of the Godhead, God the Son. Why send the Son of God? His blood in the vessel of man is so powerful, that by simply believing in His sacrifice, we are redeemed, rescued from the enemy. Talk about a Hero who was willing to lay down His life for the sake of rescuing others, God spared no expense. This is the essences of true love, God's love toward us.

Acts 4: 12, John 10: 11
"Nor is there salvation in any other, for there is no other name under heaven given among men by which we must be saved (rescued).*"*
"I, (Jesus) *am the good shepherd. The good shepherd gives His life for the sheep."*

There is no other name, no other rescuer, no other hope, but Jesus Christ, the Lord and King of all!
God is in the rescue business. He will answer the call for help, the prayer that is prayed in faith, every time we call upon the name of the Lord. However, God wants us to learn from our drowning experience, so we will not drown again. God wants us to stand secure on the solid rock of His word, where no storm or flood can carry us out to the sea of sin. Any good parent will answer the cry for help from their child who calls upon them. However, a good parent will also need to teach the child, direct the child from an error that will lead them in danger. God also wants to teach us, God loves us and has rescued us with His life.

John 10:9
If anyone enters by Me (Jesus), *he will be saved..."*

Our Provider

Genesis 22: 7 & 8
But Isaac spoke to Abraham his father and said, "My father!"
And he said, "Here I am my son." Then he said, "Look, the
fire and the wood, but where is the lamb for the burnt
offering?" And Abraham said, "My son, God will provide for
Himself the lamb for the burnt offering."
John 1: 29
The next day John (the Baptist), *saw Jesus coming toward*
him, and said, "Behold! The Lamb who takes away the sin of
the world!"

God provided a way to restore the loss relationship between
man and divinity. God provided a way so man could have
his sins washed away, the sin that permanently stained his
spirit. God provided a way where we could know and
understand something about the Creator who with a word
called the universe into existence. God provided a hope
where we can look past this life into the never-ending future
of eternity. God provided an eternal home that awaits us
when it is our time to leave our earthly dwelling. God
provided us with a peace that does not make logical sense,
yet it protects our minds against the evils in this world. God
provided us with a channel called prayer, so we could call
on the Creator, and He hears us. God provided us with His
Spirit who makes a bond with our spirits, assuring us eternal
life with Him. God provided us with a way to Himself. For in
any destination, or anything you would want to do, there is a
way to go and a way to do it. There is also a way to reach
God. God provided that way for us to live with Him forever.
 Some people might say that they do not need God for any
of the things in this life or the life after.

Proverbs 14:12
There is a way that seems right to a man, but in the end, it
leads to death.

God tells us that He has provided a way to life, a way to Himself, a way to eternity with Him. Some people might think that they can go their own way, but God says that way will lead to death. Not death of these bodies, because we all know that one day these bodies will give out, but God is talking about the death of our spirits. You say you have a better way. There is no better way! There is only one way. God provided away to His heart; Jesus Christ is the only way. Why would we want another way, other than the way that has already been given by the mercy of God, who is our Provider?

Now if God has provided all the necessities for our eternal redemption, why do we doubt that He is able to provide the needs for this temporary life, here in these earthly tents. Common sense would tell us that if God is able and willing to provide our eternal reservations with Him in paradise, why should it be hard for him to provide for our temporary needs, not all our wants, but our needs.

I spoke with a man the other day about how God provides for His creation, this includes us. The man said, "God helps those who help themselves." A commonly known statement, but it is not from God. This statement implies that God will only help those who are able to meet life's challenges. Contrary to what man thinks, God tells us throughout His word that He helps those who help others, not just themselves. Job's fortunes were not restored until he prayed for the forgiveness of his friends.

Job 42:8
And the Lord restored Job's losses when he prayed for his friends.

We see that when Job's prayers were not self- centered, then the Lord restored his losses. Job did not work harder for his losses; they were restored by the Lord. Nevertheless, God did use other people to do it. Does this mean that we do not have to work and be productive in this life?

Genesis 2: 5 & 2:15
For the Lord God had not caused it to rain on the earth, and
there was no man to till the ground.
Then the Lord God took the man and put him in the Garden
of Eden to tend and keep it.

There should be no doubt that God intended man to work
from the very beginning since He commands Adam to *tend*
the garden. I know we all have these images of Adam and
Eve sitting beneath a waterfall, eating grapes and coconut
custard pie while petting their pet lion. There is nowhere in
the Scriptures that states that Adam and Eve just sort of
loafed around all day picking fruit off of trees. We do know
that God also worked six days and rested on the seventh
day. Therefore, work is a good thing. God is productive and
wants us to be productive with the valuable give of life that
He has given us. We do not know the details of a day in the
life of Adam and Eve; however, we do know that whatever
Adam was doing, God felt that he needed a helper to assist
him in doing it.

Genesis 2:18
And the Lord God said, "It is not good for man to be alone: I
will make him a helper comparable to him."

Man needed a companion, and a helper. If Adam was just
sitting around all day collecting fruit, then Adam would not
have needed a helper to do that. However, when Adam and
Eve disobeyed God's direct orders, then the job got a lot
harder. For up until that day, God's favor and blessing were
on the couple. However, with disobedience came a curse
that replaced the blessing.

Genesis 3: 18
And you shall eat the herb of the field. In the sweat of your
face you shall eat of it.

They were thrown out of the garden, out of the place where the blessings of God had been, and into the same place where the curse of the devil is now. All those who believe have been redeemed from that curse through the blood of Jesus Christ. Nevertheless, as Adam and Eve started out with the blessings of God, we also start out with the blessing of Jesus Christ at the moment that we are born again. This does not mean that we do not have to work anymore, but it does means that God's blessings will be on all that we do, according to His will, just as it was with Adam and Eve.

Proverbs 12:11, 13: 11
He who tills his land will be satisfied with bread.
...But he who gathers by labor will increase.

God will bless what we do; however, we are required to do something. The difference is God's blessings upon or lives even in times of trouble. We have all faced battles in our lives that are a direct attack from evil. Without faith in the supernatural intervention of God, there is no hope against these attacks. Moreover, the Scriptures tell us that anything we do that is not in faith is sin, and Satan uses sin.

Romans 14:23
For whatever is not from faith is sin.

Therefore, faith is the requirement for the intervention of God to be present in our lives. If we exercise our faith in the word of God, God will back His promises as our Lord, our Savior and our Provider, even in the natural. Jesus gives us a great insight on how to live by faith.

Matthew 6: 30
"Now if God so clothes the grass of the field, which is thrown into the oven, will He not much more clothe you, you of little faith?"

Jesus is not telling us that we can sit around and expect God to send a check to us every week for having faith. Remember, Adam was assigned to *tend* the garden. Jesus is saying, as we read further in the chapter that we should not worry about our supply of food and clothes. Where there is worry in our lives, there is an absence of faith. We know that anything we do in worry or fear is not in faith, but in doubt and this is sin. In the above question, Jesus addresses the ones that worry and fear, as someone that has weak faith. However, Jesus does tell us that if we seek the kingdom of God first in faith, our needs will not be a problem. Is not God our Provider?

Philippians 4: 19
And my God will supply all your needs according to His riches by Christ Jesus.

The Apostle Paul received a great revelation on the mercy and faithfulness of God in Jesus Christ. Notice how the apostle tells us that we have riches that are available in the authority of the Lord Jesus. The apostle makes it a point to mention that our needs will be fulfilled by faith according to the abundant supply in Christ Jesus. He does not say our every desire, but our needs will be given by working in faith. King David writes the same message in different words.

Psalm 23: 1
The Lord is my Shepherd; I shall not want (lack).

Can we trust God to supply our needs according to His riches? If we can trust God for our eternal salvation, the redeeming power of His love, then why do we stumble about the thought that God will supply for our needs?

Isaiah 41: 13
For I the Lord your God, will hold your right hand, saying to you, 'Fear not, I will help you.'

As the young child who begins their first steps on unstable legs, with a firm grip on their parents hands, so God assures us that He will hold our right hand as we take steps of faith. Moreover, in faith there is no fear, so God commands us to fear not. If we are willing to work by faith and trust God with every cell of our being, then God tells us that He will help us. This again tells us that we have a responsibility to do work and God will help us according to His will. Nevertheless, God will provide the strength, the faith, the courage, the light and the path to accomplish His plan for our lives, if we believe. A great example of this is when God parted the waters of the Red Sea as Moses led the people of God from out of the land of captivity. Moses and the people had a responsibility to walk through the parted waters. God did not carry them, but He did part the waters and hold their hands through the supernatural move of His command. Moreover, God will do the same for us.

Job 38: 1 & 41
Then the Lord answered Job out of a whirlwind, and said: "Who provides food for the raven, when its young ones cry to God, and wander about for lack of food?"

God never really gives an explanation to Job as to why calamity came upon his entire life. Instead, God asked Job a number of questions that helps reveal to us His character. One of those questions is about how God provides food for the ravens. God told Job that the young ravens cry out to Him; He hears them and provides their need for food. It is strange how the ravens know enough to cry out to God for their lack. Jesus answers the question presented to Job.

Matthew 6:26
Look at the birds of the air, for they neither sow nor reap nor gather into barns; yet your heavenly Father feeds them.

God is not comparing us with the birds. However, He is telling us that He is our Provider for the needs of this life and these provisions are in Christ Jesus. Is God saying that we should be care free like the birds that do not sow, reap or gather? God has already told us that we must work, but what He is telling us is that though we are required to plant and harvest (work), God will still provide the means, so our work will not be in vain. If we follow God's instructions, mercy and blessing will follow us in our homes, at our jobs and all the days of our lives in every thing that we do. Jesus tells us that we can trust God to be our Provider in the natural by faith.

Matthew 6: 26
Are you not of more value than they?

Jesus challenges our faith with a question; are we worth more to God than the birds? If we cannot answer this question without doubts, then we do not understand His love for us. After all, when we love someone, our reaction is to give to that one we love. The reason why many relationships go sour is because the persons in the relationship are no longer willing to give to one another. The giving in love dies, therefore, the relationship dies. Job gave his prayers for his friends and was then restored twice as much as he had. God helps those who help others!

Isaiah 43:20 & 44:3
Because I give (provide), *waters in the desert, to give to My people, My chosen.*

The Prince of Life

John 6: 35, 51
And Jesus said to them, "I am the bread of life. He who
comes to Me shall never hunger, and he who believes in Me
shall never thirst."
"I am the living bread"

There are times when we go through this life with just an
existing frame of mind. We work and buy in an attempt to
raise our standard of living. We work more to buy more,
never realizing that our inner condition has never changed.
If I could only buy that, it would make my life richer. If I
could only make more money, so I could live in a bigger
house, it would make me feel alive. Think about some of the
things we do to better our lives, but somehow we continue to
come up short. When we finally buy what we always
wanted, we begin thinking about what to buy next. This is all
an attempt to fill our lives with everything else, except with
the true life of the Spirit. It seems odd that we would try to
obtain more life with things that have no life in them. God is
the Author of all life. Why would we look any place else in
search of more life?

John 6:48
"I am the bread of life"...

It is the living bread of the Holy Spirit, that fills the spirits of
all who are willing to trust God through His Son Jesus
Christ. These are words of pure Spirit because it is in the
spirit of a person that life exists. Our bodies are only a
vessel to contain the spirit. Moreover, Jesus is the very
substance of life, the life source of our spirits. Without food
our bodies will be unable to function and rebuild, they will
break down and decay. Our spirits work in a similar fashion,
with no spiritual nutrition from the only source, which is God;
our spirits fall into death. This does not mean that our spirits
no longer exist without the source of life. It does mean that

the spirit who has chosen to refuse life with God is in a dead condition already without knowing it. Without the *bread of life*, the spiritual life source that is God, the spirit will exist apart from God. God is the center of all life; we cannot begin to even imagine what true separation from God is like since no one who presently lives here on this earth has ever experienced it.

John 6:63
It is the Spirit who gives life; the flesh profits nothing. The words that I speak to you are spirit, and they are life.

Jesus being the life source, try to think in terms with something that we can relate with. The car, plane, train or ship, without the power source of fuel is useless, unable to perform the task that it was designed for as transportation. The fuel, the power source is the essential ingredient in igniting the motors to drive the machines that were manufactured to transport us safely and quickly. Without Jesus Christ, the *bread of life*, the power source of our spirits, we are as an automobile with no fuel, unable to perform the task that we were originally designed for, which is to know, serve and worship God.
Jesus said that the flesh profits nothing. Without the Spirit of God, who gives birth to our spirits, like the automobile without the fuel, we are useless in fulfilling our spiritual design. Jesus speaks about the *bread of life*, but He also speaks about the *living water*.

John 4:10
Jesus answered and said to her, "If you knew the gift of God and whom it is who says to you, give me a drink, you would have asked Him, and He would have given you living water".

Jesus again is speaking about the source of all life, for He is the *Prince of life*. Jesus as the *living bread,* gives the *living water*, which is the Holy Spirit, for the Spirit of God is life.

How can we really experience true life if we distance ourselves from the only true source? The true bread gives life to our spirits and without it; we are mere empty shells of flesh that might look good on the outside, but are dead on the inside.

Each one of our cells has a design and a purpose for the sake of the entire body, assembled together with different functions but all with one purpose, and so is the body of Christ, which is all who believe.

John 1:4, 1ˢᵗ John 5:11
In Him was life, and the life was the light of men.
And this is the testimony; that God has given us eternal life and this life is in His Son.

Jesus, the *bread of life*, the *Prince of Life* is like natural food to our bodies. Jesus is the spiritual food, the source for our spirits, for eternal life is in Jesus Christ and apart from Him, life cannot exist. Remember that the spirit is eternal and eternal death in spiritual terms is eternal separation from God. This is the death of all deaths; it is not a non-existent state, but a state of reality without God.

1ˢᵗ John 5:13
These things I have written to you who believe in the name of the Son of God (Jesus Christ), *that you may know that you have eternal life.*

When the Lord Jesus told Martha that her brother Lazarus will rise after being dead in the tomb for four days, Martha replied: *"I know that he will rise again in the resurrection at the last day."* Jesus gives her a detailed revelation on resurrection and life.

John 11:25
Jesus said to her, "I am the resurrection and the life. He who believes in Me, though he may die, he shall live."

Jesus leaves no room for question on His authority over all life. Jesus is the source of life, and He gives it to those who believe. He also reassures Martha and us that even when these natural bodies begin to fall apart and cease to function; all those who believe will be alive and in the presence of God through faith in His sacrifice. The departure from this world for any believer is by no means the end of life, but the beginning of life in eternity with the Lord Jesus Christ. Jesus, the Author of life, gives us His word on it. Is there some other way to obtain eternal life with God? Is there some other sacrifice that has been brought to the throne of God that will redeem humanity from sin? Is there any other life source that we might plug into for life eternal? Is there any other way to find the promise of life? Is there some other truth that we may know, so our lives will go on, past the barriers of time? Is there some other way to reach God? The Lord Jesus sets the record straight.

John 14: 6
Jesus said to him, "I am the way, the truth, and the life. No one comes to the Father except through Me."

The Sacrifice

Isaiah 53:5, 52:14, 52:10
Psalm 22:16
But He was wounded and crushed for our sins. He was beaten that we might have peace. He was whipped and we were healed.
Just as there were many who were appalled at him, His appearance was so disfigured beyond that of any man and His form marred beyond human likeness...
...They have pierced My hands and feet.
The Lord will bare His Holy Arm in the sight of all the nations, and all the ends of the earth will see the salvation of God.

Hundreds of years before the suffering of Christ, the Prophet Isaiah cries out and King David writes a Psalm. God revealed to them the sufferings of the Savior. His back was whipped until it looked like a plowed field, because the whip that the Romans used had pieces of broken bone tied to the tips. He was beaten to the point where He was unrecognizable, beat in the face with fists and clubs. Then when His body was nothing more than an open wound; bloody and raw, they nailed Him to a cross.

How could this Man be the Savior of the world when He could not even save Himself? The Son of God did not come to this world to save Himself, He came to save us by being our perfect, holy sacrifice. Save us from what? Jesus came to save us from the *wages of sin,* which is death! We are not speaking of the death of the body, but the death of the spirit, a death of eternal separation from God. Nevertheless, God had a plan from the first fall of Adam, and still has a plan to save us; His plan of salvation was to supply an eternal sacrifice for our sins, one without blemish, and one that was sinless and pure.

Isaiah 53:12
...Because He poured out His life unto death, and was numbered with the transgressors. He bore the sins of many...

Jesus the Man, born into this world, not by the will of a man, but by the will of God, was willing to sacrifice His all so He could pay the penalty for all our sins. Since sin has a cost, a price tag that reads death, someone had to pay with something that was worth much more than sin. Someone had to be willing and able to pay. Why was Jesus willing? I know this seems hard to understand, but God truly loves us. God's love is not based on our conduct; it is not based on a feeling. It is based on His very nature, which is love. God does have orders and principles that cannot be broken. However, these boundaries are established in His love. If God allowed them to be broken, the universe and all creation would be in disorder.

God had to design a way to pay for the sins of humanity, and still maintain His order and principles by the power of His word. God was and still is on a rescue mission, so He could bring us back to His original intended purpose. That purpose was to live with Him for eternity. Our original design was to live forever in the presence of God, but sin, like a cancer, turned life into death. Therefore, God had to make a way that we could once again live with Him for forever, taking sin and judgment out of the way, tearing down the dividing veil that did not permit us to enter in His presence. That way is Jesus Christ. Jesus took our punishment for our sins as the only sacrifice that could. Jesus, who is the very representation of God in human form, was without sin but was made the bearer of our sin so we could live.

Isaiah 53:6
We all, like sheep, have gone astray, each of us has turned to his own way; and the lord has laid on Him the iniquity of us all.

Romans 6:23
The wages of sin is death; but the gift of God is eternal life through Jesus Christ our Lord.

Therefore, look no further for your Redeemer. For it is Jesus the Christ, who the Father and all of heaven bear witness that He is the eternal sacrifice for our sins.

Acts 5: 31, 32
Him (Jesus), *God has exalted to His right hand to be a Prince and Savior, to give repentance to Israel and the forgiveness of sins. And we are witnesses to these things...*

What things did the apostles witness and proclaim throughout the world? Whom were they witnesses for?

Acts 4: 33
And with great power the apostles gave witness to the resurrection of the Lord Jesus.

The apostles were witnesses to the sacrifice and the resurrection of the Lord Jesus Christ from the dead, proving without a doubt with great signs and wonders that He is the final blood sacrifice for man's sin. There are some organizations that teach that they are witnesses for God the Father, or as they would interpret it, Jehovah God of the Old Testament. However, the apostles of Christ were not witnesses as the prophets of old. They were eyewitnesses to the death and resurrection of the Lord Jesus Christ from the dead, teaching that He is the eternal sacrifice, and in Him alone is the remission for our sins. The apostles were not witnesses of the law, which came through Moses, but they were witnesses to God's New Covenant of mercy, and this grace came through the sacrifice of Jesus Christ. We are no longer living in the days of the Old Covenant where the Law of God was mandated by judgment with no mercy. We have been redeemed from the law by the sacrifice of Christ, in that it is not something we earn or deserve, it is pure grace, given from God. The apostles were witnesses to this mercy, not to the prophetic law, since the law needed no witness; it was already established as the word of God.

Acts 3: 14, 15
"But you denied the Holy One and the just (Jesus Christ), *and asked for a murderer to be granted to you, and killed the Prince of Life, whom God raised from the dead, of which we are witnesses."*

Therefore, do not be fooled from those who claim to be witnesses for God as the prophets of old were witnesses and spokesmen, in whom God spoke through according to the law. We now have Jesus Christ, who is far above any prophet, who disarmed the charges of the law that was held against us. We are witnesses of this grace that fulfilled every letter of the law, which we ourselves could have never fulfilled. We could not earn or buy such grace because of our weak nature, for the grace of God needs only to be received in faith. We are witnesses to this grace.

Acts 2:32
"This Jesus God raised up, of which we are witnesses."

This is the true witness of every believer, the witness of the sacrifice through the grace of God. Our Lord did warn us about false witnesses who distort the truth to justify themselves and claim to be witnesses for God.
The true witnesses for God are those who are witnesses for Christ, and in His sacrifice and resurrection from the dead, as He lives in our hearts and sits at the right hand of the Father. The life of Jesus lives in every believer and this is the true testimony.

Acts 2:36
...God has made this Jesus, whom you crucified, both Lord and Christ.

For our true testimony is that Jesus Christ, who was put to death on a cross as a living sacrifice for the sins of the world, is alive! This is the living truth of the New Covenant and the testimony of the early church as they preached to the Jews first and then to the Gentiles. The true church is a witness to the resurrected Christ.

Romans 1: 3 – 6
Concerning His Son Jesus Christ our Lord, who was born of the seed of David according to the flesh, and declared to be the Son of God with power according to the Spirit of holiness, by the resurrection from the dead. Through Him we have received grace and apostleship for obedience to the faith among all nations for His name, among whom you are called of Jesus Christ.

Jesus is declared the final blood sacrifice for the remission of our sins by the power and testimony of the resurrection from the dead. He is the only sacrifice that can cancel the judgment against us. There is simply no other sacrifice!

Our True Friend

Proverbs 18:24
There are friends who pretend to be friends, but there is a
friend who sticks closer than a brother.

Some people come into our lives and influence us, some for
our good and some for evil. Some with honest intentions
and some with selfish motives that attempt to use us as a
means to acquire their wants. Then there are those who
truly make a difference in our lives. The kindred spirits who
offer a simple gift with no strings attached and no fine print
with conditions or mandatory regulations is a friend. This is
the definition of a true friend. Even though such a person
may be far and few between in this human experience, God
assures our hearts that not only is He the Sovereign Lord
and King of all the heavens and the earth, and not only the
Creator of all that is, but He is our friend.

Psalm 25:14
The friendship of the Lord is for those who fear them, and he
makes known to them His covenant.

The friendship of God is developed through a relationship
with His Spirit. It is through knowing and understanding a
person that we may give birth to a relationship of friendship.
How can we be true friends with someone we do not know?
God invites us into a relationship with Him, not based on our
performance, or because of who we think we are, but His
invitation is based on who He is, God is love. We have been
created for this very purpose, to know and love God
eternally.

Jeremiah 31:34
And no longer shall each man teach his neighbor, saying,
'know the Lord,' for they shall all know Me, from the least of
them to the greatest, says the Lord; "for I will forgive their
iniquity, and I will remember their sin no more."

The phrase (to know a person), signifies to be familiar with, to have direct contact with, an understanding through experience. God invites us to become involved, familiar with Him in a personal relationship, a one on one basis, even as a friend. To suggest that we cannot know the Creator, but rather only know about Him from a distance would be a direct contradiction of Scripture. This concept of a distant God questions the reason for our very existence. If we were not created to know the love of God, then that would mean we have been placed here for a lesser purpose, a shallow and less than filled life apart from the very life source of all living things.

James 2:23
And the Scripture was fulfilled which says, "Abraham believed God, and it was reckoned to him as righteousness"; and he was called the friend of God.

Is God saying that if we believe Him, then we are His friends? There is no doubt that God is moved by faith, He is drawn to the ones that puts their trust in Him and believes Him at His word. Abraham did not lead a perfect, sinless life. Abraham made some big mistakes as we all have done sometime in our lives. So, what made Abraham different in that God calls him His friend? We know that it was not Abraham's impressive baseball card with a high batting average of good deeds. It was Abraham's faith, he trusted, he believed God, and God is always pleased when He finds faith in someone's heart. Abraham was called a friend of God because he believed God; we can also be God's friends.

Romans 4:23, 24
Now it was not for his (Abraham's), alone that it was imputed to him, but also it shall be imputed to us who believe in Him who raised up Jesus our Lord from the dead.

Abraham was not the only one whom God referred to as a friend. We read about another man that believed God. Like Abraham, the man did not live a perfect, sinless life, yet faith was birth in him. This man also learned as Abraham did through believing God's word, that God can be trusted as a true friend. God dealt with their shortcomings, but saw their faith and their faith gave birth to a friendship with God. After all, if there is not trust in a friendship, then there is not a friendship.

Exodus 3: 11
So the Lord spoke to Moses face to face, as a man speaks to a friend

We are also invited to be friends with God by simply believing God at His word. What a privilege and honor that God has given to us, to call us His friends. We would be so grateful to have a friendship with a famous or prominent person. We would love to invite them in our homes and hear them speak about their experiences. They would have our undivided attention as they told us about whatever it was that made them successful. Moreover, here we have the opportunity to know in a friendship relationship the Creator of the universe. If we really stopped for a minute to think about this, it staggers our minds. After all, God knows everything about me, He knows all my errors, my shortcomings, my times of stupidity, and He still wants to be friends with me? What do I have to offer to this friendship? Well, let me see now, I have my sin; my unfaithfulness, my lack of wisdom and of course I have my pride. What does God offer to the friendship? He brings faithfulness, forgiveness, honesty and pure love. God would have to be crazy to be my friend! That right, God is crazy, crazy about us. After all, there is no logic in love. We cannot attempt to make sense of love; it is something that we know little about when we realize how much God loves us.
If we are willing to believe God and act on His word, we then have a friendship with God. Jesus also tells us that He is our

friend. What could be more valuable then that? Jesus Christ is our Savior, Lord, Redeemer, Provider and our hope for eternity. However, Jesus tells us that He is also our friend and we are His if we truly believe His word. Jesus also tells us that true friendship is built on the foundation of love and trust, and at times, we might have to sacrifice something for the sake of that love. Our Lord Jesus knew this first hand.

John 15: 13, 14, 15
"Greater love has no one than this, than to lay down one's life for his friends. You are My friends if you do whatever I command you."
… But I have called you friends.

Proverbs 17:17
A friend loves at all times.

Faith in Him

Habakkuk 2:4
...But the just shall live by His Faith...

What is faith? Can we be justified by faith? God says that someone who lives by faith is just. If we really want to understand faith, there is no better place in the word of God than the book of Hebrews. God answers all our questions about what is faith and how faith works through the pen of an apostle, which could be the Apostle Paul.

Hebrews 11:1
Now faith is the substance of things hoped for, the evidence of things not seen.

Do we need faith in something that we can see? No! I do not need faith to know that I am writing on a desk. I can see the desk and feel the desk. Faith is the substance, the matter, and the essence of hope that is unseen.
Now this hope, although unseen, is not a hope of not knowing, but a hope of knowing. The world uses the word hope in a not knowing term. How many times have we heard someone say, 'we will hope for the best?' That is a question of not knowing and not a statement of knowing. Are we talking about knowing future events? Not in detail, but we know what God has promised in His word concerning all those who trust Him. Therefore, we can be confident that even though we do not know the exact details of any given situation, we know when all is said and done, God will work all things for good to those who love Him. Knowing the details for our future would do us more harm than good. We have a hope of knowing, even without the details, that God is our Savior in every circumstance. The more we know of God's word, the more we will have a knowing hope, which is faith!

Romans 10:17
So faith cometh by hearing, and hearing by the word of God.

God says that we need to hear the evidence, the testimony of the word of God to have faith in Him. Without the word of God, we have no reference point for our faith. How can we have a knowing hope of faith if we do not know what God has promised in His word? If we know the promises of God, and are willing to make a decision to follow His instruction, then mountain-moving faith is ours!

Hebrews 11:2
For by it the elders obtained a good testimony.

Every page in God's word is a witness of testimony, the evidence that God is, as all the men and women who testify that God is true through the Scriptures. Faith is a knowing, and understanding that needs no physical proof because the evidence is in the heart, and out of the heart the mouth speaks, which is the testimony of all the men and women who love God. Physical matter does not limit faith, yet physical matter can be changed by faith.

Hebrews 11:3
By faith we understand that the worlds were framed by the word of God, so that the things which are seen were not made of things which are visible.

The above text clearly states that natural forces did not make themselves, but were created by the invisible word of God. Now faith is of the spirit, therefore, we cannot seek spiritual vision through physical eyes. The spiritual realm is unseen while we are in these bodies. Faith is unseen and hope is unseen. However, the spirit is a very real and a powerful active force. We read the bible in faith and not only with our physical eyes and minds, but with believing hearts. God's word needs to be absorbed as nutrients for our spirits. When this occurs, trusting God at His word becomes seen in the eyes of our understanding, and then in the natural. Any promise given from God will happen if we can understand how to live, not by physical sight, but by faith. Jesus was and is moved by faith, drawn to faith. He cannot just walk away from it. Some people place their faith in other people. Some people place their faith in money and material things. Some people place their faith in themselves, thinking that they have enough wisdom to direct their own lives. God is not moved by any other faith unless it is faith in Him alone. He is not willing to compromise His truth for our errors of false worship, which is exactly what we do when we place our faith in anything or anybody else beside God. God is not only talking about making some symbol out of wood, stone or gold and kneeling down before it to worship. The real question is where do we place our trust? We know so many people who truly believe that if they had enough money, all their problems would be over, but they deceive themselves.

Hebrews 11: 7, 8, 10, 20-23, 31, 32
By faith Noah, by faith Abraham, by faith Sarah, by faith Isaac, by faith Jacob, by faith Joseph, by faith Moses, by faith the harlot Rahab, Gideon, Barak, Samson, and also David and Samuel and the prophets.

By faith, by believing the message from God with a confident hope, every one of the above began to take steps by faith, and even some took leaps.

Hebrews 11:39
And all these, having obtained a good testimony through faith, did not receive the promise...

Now they had obtained many promises, but God reveals to writer that the Promise, Jesus Christ was to come later. The Promise was given to Abraham, to Moses, and to other prophets, but they saw Him from afar. They left here not seeing the Savior come into the world. However, in a confident hope, they testified of the day, seeing it in the spirit as if it had already taken place.

Now all believers, as Abraham, are called to move in an act of faith.

Galatians 3:8
And the Scripture, foreseeing that God would justify the Gentiles by faith, preached the Gospel to Abraham beforehand, saying, "In you all the nations shall be blessed."

God tells us that in the Seed of Abraham, all nations will be blessed, because it was through his Seed that the Promise is planted in the soil of hearts. The seed of the faith was spoken through the prophets until it was time for the Promise to be born in the natural.

Galatians 4:4
But when the fullness of the time had come, God sent forth His Son, born of woman, born under the law.

So the Promise of God became seen in the natural at the birth of Christ Jesus.

Now man defines faith as a belief without proof. However, the proof that God is real is not only in our hearts, but also in the creation itself.

Now faith is the raw matter that holds all things together by the word of God. As Abraham and Noah, Enoch and Moses, we have been called to live in the same faith. We have been born in the family of faith. The very substance of faith lives in us, if we believe.

John 4
For everyone born of God overcomes the world. This is the victory that has overcome the world, even our faith.

There should be no doubt, no question in this promise given to the Apostle John, that we will always overcome, live, stand, walk and run in victory with faith in God's word. This issue must be settled before ever attempting a step in faith. For all those who have come to the throne of God, by Jesus Christ, have been given the inheritance of faith. The same power that raised Jesus from the dead and has already raised us from a spiritual death, that same power of God lives in all that believe in Christ Jesus as Lord and Savoir. There is only one definition for the word faith. It is simply trusting God at His word, and becoming a living action of that trust. Living our lives based on the warnings and promises of God will cause each one of us to stand with Abraham, Noah, Isaac, Jacob, Joseph, Moses, and Sarah. The list goes on and on, all written in the Book of Life, not because of keeping the law to the letter, but because of keeping their faith. God also has given all of us a measure of faith. Our faith account is full and can never be overdrawn, because it has been purchased with something much more valuable than gold or silver. It was bought with blood, and not just any blood, but sinless holy blood that was spilled on the cross for us. Should we take such a gift as the redemption of our souls so casual? The life of faith is a living testimony that God is real and He rewards those who seek Him by faith. However, without faith, we are dead, spiritually bankrupt, and separated from God. There is simply no way that someone can fake faith. It is in a person's life by the power of the Holy Spirit, or it is not.

2nd Peter 1:5
But also for this very reason, giving all diligence, add to your faith virtue, to virtue knowledge, to knowledge self control, to self control perseverance, to perseverance godliness, to godliness brotherly kindness, and to brotherly kindness love.

The Holy Spirit reveals to Peter that on the foundation of our faith, God can transform our thinking, renew our minds, and add virtue, self-control, kindness and love to our faith, and by our faith. What did Jesus have to say about faith?

Matthew 17:2
I say to you, if you have faith as a mustard seed, you will say to this mountain, move from here to there, and it will move; and nothing will be impossible for you.

Jesus tells us that with such a small amount of faith we can move the biggest mountains in our lives. He tells us that with faith, the impossible becomes possible for those who believe.
Jesus touched the eyes of a blind man and said, *"According to your faith let it be to you," (Matthew 9:29).* Faith is the conduit to bring fourth the things unseen.

John 14:12
Jesus answered: "I tell you the truth; anyone who has faith in Me will do what I have been doing."

Now when Jesus spoke these words, He was speaking about the evidence of miracles, the moving of mountains, trusting in the power of God. Jesus makes this very clear when He said, *"Anyone who has faith in Me"....* Notice Jesus said, *"Anyone!"* Not just a chosen few, not just leaders in the church, but *anyone.* That means you and I, who place our faith in Jesus, can do the things Jesus has done. Notice how Jesus says that our faith must be in Him, and not in the church, not in the pastor, but in Him.

Hebrews 11:6
Without faith, it is impossible to please Him (God).

We might be able to please our parents, please our spouses, and please our bosses, our friends, and our children, and so on without faith. God tells us not to even attempt to please God without faith. Do not bother coming to God in prayer and in an assembly without faith. You are wasting your time. For if we do not believe that God is more than able to perform His word, then do not bother putting on the mask of religion in order to impress other people. If we are unwilling to take the very life of God's word in our daily lives, then we are simply practicing rituals.

Hebrews 12:2
...Looking unto Jesus, the Author and Finisher of our faith.

If we are unwilling to look unto Jesus Christ as our faith source, then our faithless prayers will be vain words meant only to satisfy those around us. God requires that we come to Him, not by sight, not by feelings and not by logic, but by faith, trusting His word, knowing He is able to do all that He has said. God is faithful in all He has promised. Jesus gives us a complete outline of the outcome of a person's life when it is lived in faith, trusting in God.

Luke 6:47, 48
Whoever comes to Me, and hears My sayings (words), and does them, I will show you whom he is like. He is like a man who dug deep and laid the foundation on the rock. And when the flood arose, the stream beat vehemently against the house, and could not shake it, for it was founded on the rock.

Jesus tells us that in this life, we would be wise to place our faith in Him. The person who places their faith in Jesus Christ is like a man building a house. This house, built with the substance of faith, anchored on a solid Rock of Christ, cannot be moved by the storms of this life. Jesus also tells us that when the flood arose and the water beat against the house, it did not fall. Notice how Jesus said, "W *hen the flood arose,"* not if the flood arose, which means floods will come in this life. It is not a matter of if, but when.

Therefore, do not think we can live without faith, because the floods will show us what our houses are really made of. If they are made of faith, the unseen matter of trust in Christ, then your house will not fall no matter how much the wind, storms, and floods of this life beat against it. We will stand on a firm foundation of the solid Rock, who is the King of all kings. The evidence of this is and always will be the testimony of our lives in times of crisis.

Romans 10:17
So then faith comes by hearing, and hearing by the word of God.

We cannot expect our faith to grow by watching the 6:00 o'clock news, by watching and reading every sport event that is played, or by working 16-hour days. As the carpenter must labor to build the house, so we are required to seek God through His word. Yes, it does take some effort. After all, while the rest of the world chases after the temporal pleasures of this life and ignores the love of God, we who believe should be pressing toward our eternal dwelling that awaits all people with faith. This is by no means saying that we should live as a monk somewhere in the mountains of Italy, yet we are in the world, but not of the world. There is nothing wrong with good things that provide our comfort, but we cannot place our faith in them, instead of placing our faith in the living God. Is not God able to supply all of our needs in Christ Jesus?

Romans 10:11
For the Scriptures say, no one who puts his faith in Him will ever be put to shame.

Anyone who trusts in God, will not fall into the dark pit of shame. Even in times of hardship and sorrow, when the problems of this life are crashing against us, yet by faith we can trust in the words of our wonderful Savior Jesus Christ.

Revelation 22:12
And behold, I am coming quickly...

Therefore, since we know that Jesus will return in all His glory, we should live this life with the shield of faith.

Ephesians 6:16
Above all, taking the shield of faith with which you will be
able to quench all the fiery darts of the wicked one.

Our faith is our shield, a protective device to stop the
enemy's invasion with doubt. Remember we do have an
enemy! This enemy has only two objectives on his mind and
that is to destroy every human soul on this planet and
discredit God. He will use anything or anybody he can to
derail the believer and prevent someone from knowing the
truth of Jesus Christ as Savior. Therefore, God tells us to
live with the shield of faith before us.

Hebrews 12:2
Let us fix our eyes on Jesus, the Author and Finisher of our
faith, who for the joy set before Him endured the cross,
scorning its shame, and sat down at the right hand of the
throne of God.

Jesus Christ is the *Author and Finisher of our faith, so* let us
look at that Perfect Letter and copy our lives to His. We hear
the voice of Jesus throughout the Scriptures and in our
hearts asking us repeatedly:

Matthew 8:26
"Why are you fearful, O' you of little faith?"

Jesus had a lot to say about faith; He recognized great faith
and questioned weak faith. Jesus saw where faith had
abounded and where it was not.
Jesus taught that if we have faith the size of a small seed,
we could move mountains. Now I know our minds will say,
'no,' but God says,' yes,' and He is higher than our thoughts.
Faith will break through the limitations of our minds; God's
power is far beyond our reasoning.
There are many times when God says, *'Fear not.'* What He
is really saying is, 'trust Him', for there is no place for fear
when faith is present. Just as darkness must leave when the

presence of light enters, so fear has no place in faith. When faith is matured in a human spirit, it is a spiritual bolt of lightning that God will not ignore. Jesus asked this question repeatedly.

Mark 4:40
"Why are you so fearful? How is it you have no faith?"

When all hell has broken out around me, when the valley begins to get so low it becomes dark, and all those around me start to ask, what are you going to do? I remember the words of Jesus our Savior, *"Why are you so fearful? How is it you have no faith?"* If Jesus Christ is our Savior, (and He is), then instead of running around in worry, what we really need to do is continue to run forward in faith. Therefore, we are not shaken by the attacks of the enemy, but we are focused and rooted on the word of God. For if God is for us (and He is for those who believe in Him) then what enemy can come against us? If we are willing to break through the veil, into our inner most part of faith, then God will give us a revelation of Himself that we could never imagined in our farthest thoughts. If we are willing to take that step according to the word that He has already spoken, then God will respond with revelation and blessings. God wants to reveal Himself to us, and undoubtedly bless us with all the riches in Christ Jesus. God loves us, and He has already given us the wonderful gift of eternal life by the sacrifice of His Son, Jesus Christ.

Faith is required to receive the gift of salvation, the blessing of God, and the revelation of His very nature. Without faith, we are like a fallen runner who is just sitting while other runners pass us by.

There is no other name in that our lives can be empowered with the very resurrection power that raised Jesus from the dead. There are no other options of placing our faith in saints or mere men of the past, present or future. All the apostles knew where to place their faith, but God expressed it the best through a man who at one time was determined to stop the faith in Jesus Christ.

Galatians 2:20
And the life which I live now in the flesh I live by faith in the Son of God, (Jesus Christ) *who loved me and gave Himself for me.*

The Word

Psalm 1: 1
Blessed are the undefiled in the way, who walk in the law of the Lord.

God created the earth and the heaven by the word that proceeded from Him. His word is the very reason why we exist. His word is life, and can make a dramatic difference in our lives. One of the best places in the revelation of God to discover the depth of His word is in the book of Psalms. The man whom the Holy Spirit used to take notes in Psalm 119 is unknown, but whoever it was, God showed him the hidden secrets of His word. The Holy Spirit begins with establishing the benefits of following God's instruction in the Psalm.

Psalm 119: 34
Give me understanding according to Your word.

Throughout the Psalm, we will see the words *His law, concept, precept, statutes, commandments; testimonies and His way*; all used to describe the word of God. The bottom line is that anything that God says in His word, whether in a commandment, a testimony or a precept is His expression and revelation to us.

Psalm 119 1: 2
Blessed are those who keep His testimonies.

God opens the Psalm by telling us that there are blessings for all those that keep His word. Let us not get religious in saying that by keeping His commandments redeems us from the eternal judgment of sin. That is not what God is saying. He is telling us that there are great rewards in following His instruction in this life. Why should there not be? God knows what He is doing and we do not. I know we all think that we know what we are doing, but just look at the world in the current state of corruption, murder and deceit.

People ask, 'why does God allow these things to happen?' God gave us the earth, the fish, the birds, and everything else to use. Everything on the earth has been given to man to enjoy and care for. God also gave us a free will. The question is not, how could God let this happen, but how could we let this happen to ourselves. The answer is simple, sin! A sensitive subject when dealing with the failure of humanity, nevertheless, it is true. Once we start talking about sin, judgment and eternal punishment, most people's defensives go up and they feel like someone is pointing a finger at them. However, sin has stripped us of our understanding the word of God. Sin has separated us from the Creator; therefore, we became lost, shortsighted and at times, ignorant concerning what God said. God's instruction is for our own good since we do not realize how much sin has corrupted the soul of man. It has distorted his thoughts. It is not a matter of restriction, but protection.

1st Peter 2: 7
They stumble, being disobedient to the word...

There is no controversy that sin is the failure of man. The definition of sin is disobedience to what God has already said. Sin is also our error of doubt, choosing to believe a lie instead of God's truth. When God commands us to do what He says, and we decide not to do it, sin is present in our lives. Can there be blessings in sin? How can God bless the very thing that separates us from Him? God will not bless unrighteousness and corruption; He is against the criminal actions that are against humanity.
Can the world ever change from the dominant presence of sin, luring people with greed, selfishness and temporary pleasures? There is only one hope for this world and that is to understand and follow God's instruction. God gave us a manual; His promises are written in His book and are there to guide our walk through this temporary experience and into eternity. There is only one way, an avenue that is to be taken in understanding and acting on God's word.

A prominent teacher of Israel, a Pharisee came to Jesus by night to question Him on His message. Jesus gives this man the first step in discovering God's plan for transforming a person from the domain of sin, into the kingdom of God.

John 3: 3
Jesus answered and said to him, "Most assuredly, I say to you, unless one is born again, he can see the kingdom of God."

This bold statement caused the Pharisee to stumble in his understanding. However, God speaks clearly in explaining the principle of salvation and transformation. Unless the very nature of a person is changed from the bondage of sin to the freedom of righteousness, we cannot even see (understand), the kingdom of God, no less enter in to it. Jesus is speaking of the *eyes of our understanding,* the vision of our spirits. This change can only come from within the spirit, by the awesome Spirit of God. Jesus was not giving the Pharisee a lesson in self-help improvement. This transformation can only be performed by the power of God and only then can a person begin living in the blessing of the kingdom of God. Is that to say that other people, non-believers do not receive the blessings of this life?

Matthew 5: 45
"For He makes His sun rise on the evil and on the good, and sends rain on the just and on the unjust."

Material blessing can certainly come to those who continually walk away from God. However, His blessing of peace, His blessing of eternal redemption and His blessing of love will not be with those that are against to His word. The world may enjoy the natural blessing of God's creation for only a short season, but time is running out quickly. Jesus gives us a wonderful illustration on the sin of man and the patience of God toward those that are willing to follow His instruction.

Matthew 13: 24, 25
"The kingdom of heaven is like a man who sowed good
seed in His field; but while men slept, his enemy came and
sowed tares among the wheat and went his way."

The field of man is his heart. This is where the word of God is planted, or the seed of sin is planted, both in the spirit of a man. God had sowed only good things in the heart of Adam and Eve. However, the enemy had sowed a tare, a seed of doubt in their hearts that caused them to sin, the very disobedience that has taken root in our nature. Jesus tells us that it was while they slept, He is not taking about the physical rest required by our natural bodies. Rather, He is speaking of a spiritual slumber, an unawareness of the enemy's deceitfulness that had caused Adam and Eve to lose the very best that God had planned for them. We also can lose the very best that God has for us if we live in a spiritual slumber to His instruction. Jesus goes on to explain the outcome of the tares and the wheat.

Matthew 13:26
"But when the grain had sprouted and produced a crop, then
the tares also appeared."

This statement is a powerful lesson within itself. The sin in our lives will eventually surface, although it may appear that we have gotten away with it for a while. Jesus tells us here that it will show up in time. As the tares needed to grow with the wheat to be identified, so our sin will grow and will become noticeable by our words, the actions we take and the poor decisions that we make. We cannot cover up sin, or simply act as though it does not exist; we will see it as in the current news headlines, as we witness a world full of corruption and hate. There is only one way to remove sin, and that is to wash it away by the blood of Jesus Christ. There is no other substitute for His eternal sacrifice for sin.

Nothing has the power to cleanse our spirits from the eternal stain of sin that has infected our spirits.

Matthew 13: 28, 29
"He (the man that sowed the wheat), *said to them* (his servants), *'An enemy has done this.' The servants said to him, 'Do you want us then to go and gather them* (the tares), *up?' "But he said, 'No, lest while you gather up the tares you also uproot the wheat with them.' "*

Jesus identifies two very important truths in this Scripture. The first is that we have an enemy! We are not talking about the Hollywood entertainment productions about remaining spirits that go through walls and scare the mortals around them as we spoke about in the previous chapter. We are not talking about a fabricated studio set where the imaginations of men are manifested to an almost realistic state. We have an enemy that is not looking to entertain, but to destroy us, to kill the very life that abides in our spirits. He will certainly use the means of entertainment and anything else that is available in his deception. His objective is not for our amusement, but for our destruction. He is looking to destroy our lives here with sorrow, bitterness and resentment, and to steal our eternal hope for everlasting life with God in paradise. He does not take this task lightly, he is relentless in his pursuit and will not give up his fight.
The second truth is the merciful nature of God. Jesus tells us that rather then disturb the purity of the wheat (those that believe in Him), He will allow the tares (those that have rejected Him), to grow together and even reap the benefits of His creation. Why do we see a world that is captivated by evil, and yet, it still enjoys the benefits of God's work? Jesus gave us the answer in the above text. Moreover, remember that the blessings that the world enjoys now are only for a very short time. It is only a grain of sand compared to the never-ending shores of eternity. Nevertheless, Jesus does show us the outcome of those that are willing to trust Him and those that reject His word of mercy.

Matthew 13:30
'Let both grow together until harvest, and at that time of harvest I will say to the reapers, "First gather together the tares and bind them in bundles to burn them, but gather the wheat into my barn."

Therefore, the blessings of God creation can certainly be enjoyed by the tares of this world for now, but their hope for eternity has been stolen. However, the wheat of this life will enjoy the abundant blessing of God now and for eternity.

Psalm 1: 2, Matthew 5: 8
Blessed are those who keep His testimonies, who seek Him with the whole heart.
"Blessed are the pure in heart, for they shall see God."

How can we get our hearts right with God? Can we gain His favor by obeying the law given to Moses? Can we draw closer to Him by simply doing good deeds? When God speaks about the pure in heart, He is not speaking about a person that by their own will power has fulfilled the requirements of the law. He is not talking about the person that has taken oaths of poverty, oaths of celibacy, or oaths of silence. God is revealing the person whose heart (the spirit), has been washed, cleansed from the impurity of sin. This is not to say that such a person is perfect, but forgiven by God's power and His grace according to the promise of His word. It is only then that the true oath of surrender to God can be a reality in this life. It is in the spirit that God has declared us not guilty, and purity is then present. Therefore, the only way that this could ever take place is if someone was willing to pay the price for sin, and Jesus was.

Romans 5: 8
But God demonstrated His own love toward us, in that while we were still sinners, Christ died for us.

Blessed are the pure in heart, and blessed are those that seek God with their whole heart, because they are the ones that have received forgiveness by the power of His grace. Therefore, their hearts are new, born again, as Jesus explained to the Pharisee. It is only once our hearts have been cleansed from our sins, that we may see God through a pure heart with unselfish motives. Concerning this principle, Jesus gives us another illustration on how the word of God is like a seed. Faith in His word will not only result in eternal blessings, but also in the blessings of this life. For God's forgiveness from sin will affect both the spiritual and natural state of a person. Once the seed has been received and nourished, then it grows into the purity of God's love.

Luke 8:11, 12, 13, 14
"Now the parable is this: The seed is the word of God.
Those by the wayside; the devil comes and takes it away.
The ones on the rock; in time of temptation fall a way.
The ones that fell among the thorns; bring no fruit to
maturity."

Jesus tells us that the word of God is as a seed that is planted, but does not always take root due to various reasons. He goes on to show us that those that hear the word of God by the wayside have the seed stolen from their hearts. These are the ones that the seed does not take root in at all. The word of God's grace is cast aside as nonsense, and ridiculed as a hope for the weak and needy. It mocks some people that feel that if there is a God, He is removed from the daily affairs of our lives. These are the ones that the seed of God's word are simply ignored as rubbish, because the enemy has stolen the word of faith and replaced it with self-centered logic. The seed that falls on the rock is received at first, but then is given a low priority, resulting in placing everything else more important than God. In this case, the fire of faith has been reduced to a little spark that barely gives any light and eventually gives way to the storms of this life and the deceitfulness of the enemy. The seeds of faith that falls among the thorns are probably the saddest of all, since the seed does take root for a while, but is consistently drowned out by selfish motives and ambitions. The seed becomes dormant and is overshadowed by the riches and pleasures of this life.

Luke 8: 6
"Seeing they may not see, and hearing they may not understand.'

Jesus quotes the word given to the prophet Isaiah in saying that the people have forfeited their spiritual vision and hearing for trash. They traded it for the mere pennies of the temporary pleasures of this life, not realizing that God is the Giver of all blessings and that His blessings are for eternity. His blessings, His favor and His love are all given by the power of His promises in His word. It is the word of God that is sown, planted in our spirits that will give us the overcoming faith to bring us through this life and into His eternal dwelling.

Psalm 119: 26, 27
Teach me Your statutes. Make me understand the way of Your precepts; so I meditate on your wonderful works.

God's words are not just poetic verses designed to comfort us in times of need and soften the blow of life's tragedies. God's word is His unquestionable, faithful promises in divine truth that is not moved by deceptive images. Moreover, it is the positive, offensive weapon, that is given to every believer as a means of defeating every enemy that stands against God and us.

Ephesians 6:17
And take the helmet of salvation and the sword of the Spirit, which is the word of God.

Any army that will use only defensive weapons against an enemy will be doing nothing more than just occupying the ground that they have. Once an offensive weapon is introduced in the battle, the enemy is pushed back and defeated. This is the line that separates the sideline spirit and the spirit that wants to live in the victory of God's promises. This line is what divides the warriors from the bystanders that are willing just to hold their ground, not realizing that God has much more, and that there is more ground to be taken back from the enemy.

Psalm 119: 24
Your testimonies also are my delight and my counselors.

Throughout the Scriptures, we see that God has and will establish everything, every event according to His word. We read how God only spoke the word and creation burst into existence. We read how God spoke the word to Abraham with a promise to be a father of many nations. We see the promise of deliverance given to Moses as God leads His people from bondage. Moreover, we see the promise of a Savior, a Messiah that can bring all people out of the bondage of sin and into the glorious kingdom of God. All spoken by God and all happened just as He said it would. Therefore, God's word is a living testimony of what He has done and what He will do. If we confess to believe in God, then the testimony of the word of God should be our delight and our counsel. His word is where our faith should be grounded, anchored, firmly rooted, because we know that God is all truth. There is no better counsel than the word of God, there is no better advice we can act on than what God has already stated. However, to have faith in God's word, we need to know and understand the power that is within every command.

Psalm 119: 27, 28, 33, 34, 36
Make me understand... Strengthen me... Teach me... Give
me understanding... Incline my heart...

God does not tell us here just to pray for more faith, since faith comes through *hearing the word of God* and faith experiences, which all comes from God Himself, Jesus being the *Author and Finisher* of our faith, but we do need to pray for understanding and strength.

Romans 10: 17
So faith comes by hearing, and hearing by the word of God.

The word of God, who is Jesus Christ, is our faith source. It is where the faith foundation for our lives are built upon, and it is our re-fueling source supply where our faith can be charged and ready for use with maximum power. Whether we realize it or not, faith is also inspected. The enemy will challenge our faith in many situations in this life. We say that we believe in the power of God's supremacy. However, do our actions support our words? Whatever God says, He will do just as He has said. Of course, we do not know times, for God is in complete control of all time, according to His timetable and not ours.
Out of hearing and understanding the word of God, faith is manifested. Moreover, faith will change our thinking, resulting in a change of our motives and actions. Faith brings forth change, and it is always a change to bring us closer to God. It may not always be easy, but it will reap a holy reward.

Psalm 119: 11
Your word I have hidden in my heart that I might not sin against you.

The above Scripture is very powerful in the sense that we often wonder how we can prevent errors in this life. At times, it may be an old sin that re-surfaces in our path, or a new temptation that we have never faced before. There are times where abundant blessings will bring new challenges and new allurement from the world. We have seen many, including those written about in the Scriptures that had fallen from grace due to the temptation of greed, lust and self-gratification. God tells us clearly that the only way to prevent the consistent error of our earthly nature is to keep His word foremost in our hearts. Let His word be deeply rooted so that it cannot be moved by physical circumstances, as Jesus taught about the seed that falls on good soil.

Luke 8: 15
"But the ones that fell on the good ground are those who, having heard the word with a noble and good heart, keep it and bear fruit with endurance."

When God's word is heard, and the decision is made to follow it, the roots of the seed begin to grow deeper in the heart. Before long, the fruits of that seed will be present by actions of faith. It all begins with hearing and living in His word, committing to follow His instruction.

Psalm 119: 42
For I trust in Your word.

Faith is defined as trust. If we trust God's word as truth, as the undisputed fact without doubt, then faith is in motion within us. If we are going to trust God's word, we must settle the issue that it is indeed the divine revelation from God.

1st Peter 1: 20, 21
Knowing this first, that no prophecy of Scriptures is of any private interpretation, for prophecy never came by the will of man, but men spoke from God as they were moved by the Holy Spirit.

Therefore, understanding that God's word is the final authority in all creation, we can move in faith. It is the word of God that had been revealed to the prophets of old. By the word of God, they received divine instruction, warnings and blessings. Their hope was in the total authority of His promises, instructions, and warnings.

Psalm 119: 89
Forever, O Lord, Your word is settled in heaven.

The Holy Spirit revealed to the Apostle John as his gospel opens, describing the word of God as more then the supreme, divine instruction from the Creator. God reveals to the apostle that the Word actually became a Man. The Word now takes on a personal title, a bridge for a relationship.

John 1: 1, 14
In the beginning was the Word, and the Word was with God, and the Word was God.
And the Word became flesh and dwelt among us, and we beheld His glory, the glory as of the only begotten of the Father, full of grace and truth.

The spoken word of God, God's very expression of Himself, took on humanity, put on a covering of flesh and bones and lived among us. God goes on to tell us that the Word was with God the Father, as He holds all the divinity as God and came into the natural on a search and rescue mission that would no doubt change the course of man's eternal fate. The Word is Jesus Christ, who was willing to become a final blood sacrifice for the remission of man's sin. This is the very reason why simply faith in His name can save any soul from the everlasting judgment of sin. The power of the Word that was always with God and is God, became one of us, therefore, He had taken upon Himself legally, all the judgment of our sin. The Holy Spirit wasted no time in establishing the deity and the authority of the Word right from the very beginning of the gospel.
Therefore, it was the Word, Jesus Christ that was revealed to the prophets of old by the power of the Holy Spirit. The

same Word that commanded *"Let there be light",* as God began to create according to His good pleasure, is the same *Word that became flesh.* It was Jesus as the Word that was revealed as God to God fearing men and women throughout the Old Testament. It was the Word that was given to the prophets of old, and by the Word, they knew God, since the Word is and will always be God. Therefore, it was always Jesus, God the Son who was and is the bridge between God the Father and humanity.

John 1:18
No one has seen God at any time. The only begotten Son, who is in the bosom of the Father, He has declared Him.
1ˢᵗ John 5: 20
And we may know that the Son of God has come and has given us understanding that we may know Him who is true, in His Son Jesus Christ. This is the true God and eternal life.

In the books of the Old Testament, we will read many times that the word of the Lord came to a prophet. Therefore, he knew the Lord according to that word. Moses did not know the Lord until He spoke to Moses, only then did Moses know Him. We read how Samuel did not know the Lord because there was no word given to Samuel from God.

1ˢᵗ Samuel 3: 7
Now Samuel did not yet know the Lord, nor was the word of the Lord revealed to him.

The revelation of God, the expression of His will is in His word. If God never spoke, we would only know about Him through the creation that He made, but we would never know Him in a relationship, because a relationship is established through communication. Knowing God through the creation is simply, knowing that He is, as the creation is a testimony that God is the Creator of all. However, by knowing His word, we grow into to a deeper personal relationship that gives birth to a revelation of His love. Jesus was the Word that was expressed to the prophets of old, revealing the surface of the divinity of God, and is still the Word that now sits in the mist of the throne and is revealed to all that are willing to accept Him.

Revelation 19: 16, 12
And He has a robe and on His thigh a name written:
KING OF KINGS AND LORD OF LORDS
He was clothed with a robe dipped in blood, and His name is called THE WORD OF GOD.

Worship Him

Exodus 34:14
For you shall worship no other god, for the Lord, whose
name is Jealous, is a jealous God.

God, the Creator of all living things gives us a direct
command and brings us to an understanding on how He
feels about our worship. Now the Scriptures do not define
worship in the standard dictionary format. However, the
Scriptures do illustrate to us by the lives of God-fearing men
and women, the true meaning of worshiping the one and
only God of all creation.

Exodus 34:8
So Moses made haste and bowed his head toward the earth
and worshiped.

Is worshiping God just a proclamation of prayer in a certain
place at a certain time? Moses did not only bow his head
and pray to God, but he surrendered all that he had, all that
he was and placed God on the throne of his life. Moses
committed his life to the divine plan and purpose of God. In
return, God gave Moses a revelation of what it takes to truly
worship Him.

Exodus 34:13
But you shall destroy their altars, break their sacred pillars,
and cut down their wooden images.

If we are serious about worshiping God, there must be some
rearrangement of priorities in our lives. We might not have
stone altars and ivory pillars, or wooden images of animals
that we bow down to in our homes, but can we worship
other things in our lives? I believe that God was showing
Moses and us that many of our preconceived ideas of the
world are wrong, and need to be torn down in our minds.
Our faith in money, our assets, our professional status, our

education and our self images all need to be far behind the trust and faith in God, which is living worship. There is nothing wrong with the material things that God has blessed us with, but the error occurs when we worship them.

We have all heard the expression, 'the almighty dollar.' If the dollar was so almighty, it would be able to correct anything in our lives, and we know that it cannot. Just look around at some of the problems that the rich and famous have. All the money, all the assets and all the material things that one might posses could never supply the peace and total fulfillment of our existence as the manifestation of God's love in our hearts. This is where true worship is born, in the heart of every true believer.

Nevertheless, God commands our worship and is obviously very sensitive about us giving our worship to something or somebody else. God tells us loud and clear; *"For you shall worship no other god."* Jesus totally supports the command. When Satan asked for something that God alone deserves, Jesus sets the record straight.

Matthew 4: 9 &10
And He (Satan), said to Him (Jesus), "All these things I will give You if You will fall down and worship me."
*   Then Jesus said to him, "Away with you Satan! For it is written, 'You shall worship the Lord your God, and Him only you shall serve.'*

There are many interesting aspects to this conversation, but I see two that need to be focused upon concerning the subject of worship.

First, Satan wants to be worshiped as a god. It is obvious that Satan thinks he is a god. Well in some aspects of the word, he is. He does rule the hearts of many people, of course through deception, nevertheless, he does rule over some of humanity. Moreover, when Adam fell in the garden and sinned against God, he did give Satan his authority to rule over the earth. Remember, God tells us not to give our worship to any other so-called god because He is the one and only true God, we can see that Satan wants our worship because he thinks that he is a god. Image how disillusioned Satan really is because of his sin, he actually thought that Jesus would worship him.

The second interesting fact in this meeting is that we can clearly see here how sin can distort our sense of reality. Nevertheless, if Satan cannot convince us to worship him directly, he will use every lie he has in preventing us to worship God. Jesus hits Satan right between the eyes when He tells him that no one is to be worshiped except for God alone. No angel, no saint, no evil spirit, no one except God is to be worshiped, because He alone is worthy.

As we quickly discover, Jesus accepted worship. If Jesus is not God the Son, then He would be in a great contradiction by accepting any worship from man.

Matthew 8: 1&2
When He (Jesus), *had come down from the mountain, great multitudes followed Him. And behold, A leper came and worshiped Him, saying, "Lord, if You are willing, You can make me clean.'*

Did not Jesus tell Satan that God alone is to be worshiped? The text does not say that the leper cried out to Jesus or simply asked Him to heal his illness, but the leper *worshiped* Jesus. In addition, what was the Lord's response to this?

Matthew 8:3
Then Jesus put out His hand and touched him, saying, "I am willing; be cleansed."

Jesus did not rebuke the leper as He did Satan. He did not tell the leper that the Lord God alone is to be worshiped. On the contrary, Jesus accepted the leper's worship and accommodated his faith with a supernatural healing. Jesus accepted worship because He is God the Son. Now in the eyes of the Pharisees, this was blasphemy. The Pharisees taught the law and the law is; *you shall worship no other god.* Was this a one-time incident, somehow over looked in the translation of the Holy Scriptures?

Matthew 9:18
While He (Jesus) *spoke these things to them, a ruler came and worshiped Him, saying, "My daughter has just died, but come and lay Your hand on her and she will live.*

Again, we see Jesus worshipped in the presence of a multitude. Jesus, the true Teacher would surely have corrected this man if he had been in error in worshiping Him. Again, we see that Jesus accepts the man's worship and proceeds to follow the man to his daughter.

Matthew 9:19
So Jesus arose and followed him, and so did His disciples.

There are two interesting facts within this text.
The first, Jesus accepted the man's worship. Secondly, He also accepted the man's faith. The ruler claimed that if Jesus would just touch his daughter, though she was dying, she would live. Jesus stopped what He was teaching and followed the man to where his daughter was. We see this repeatedly in the gospels, how Jesus was worshiped and accepted worship as only God can, according to the command given to Moses.

Matthew 15:25
Then she came and worshiped Him (Jesus), *saying, "Lord help me."*

The most often quoted prayer in the Scriptures is a prayer we have all prayed sometime in our lives, *"Lord, help me."* We do not need a bible study to pray this prayer; this is a prayer of desperation. Nevertheless, it was a prayer that began with worship. Again, we see Jesus accept the worship and accommodate the woman's faith by a supernatural healing.

Matthew 15:28
Then Jesus answered and said to her, "O woman, great is your faith! Let it be to you as you desire."

At last, we read in the Gospel of Matthew when Mary Magdalene and the other Mary visited the tomb of Jesus on that early Sunday morning after His death. They find the stone that once covered the entrance of the tomb rolled away. They find an angel sitting on the stone, as the guards who were there to secure the tomb shook with fear and became like dead men. The angel tells the women that Jesus is not in the tomb, He has risen! The two women start back to bring this great news to the disciples, when the risen Christ meets them on the way.

Matthew 28:9
And as they went to tell His disciples, behold, Jesus met them saying, 'REJOICE!" So they came and held Him by the feet and worshiped Him.

Again, Jesus accepts their worship. Jesus did not tell them to only worship God the Father, but received their worship as God the Son. Jesus receives worship as only God can rightfully receive.
 Mathew opens his Gospel with three wise men that followed a star for the sole purpose of worshiping Jesus.

Matthew 2:2 & 11
"Where is He who has been born King of the Jews? For we (the three wise men), *have seen His star and we have come to worship Him."*
And when they (the three wise men), *had come into the house, they saw the young Child with His mother, and fell down and worshiped Him* (Jesus Christ).

Is Matthew the only writer of the Scriptures that brings this fact to light? The Scriptures have many examples of Jesus accepting worship. The writer of the Gospel of Mark tells us about demonic spirits that also worshiped Jesus, but Jesus did not accept their false worship.

Mark 5:6
When he (the demonic spirit in a man)*, saw Jesus from afar, he ran and worshiped Him. And he cried out with a loud voice. "What have I to do with You, Jesus, Son of the Most High? I implore You by God that You do not torment me.'*

The fallen, demonic angels worshiped Jesus as deity with their mouths, but not with their hearts. We could easily fall into that same trap if we are not careful in placing other things or other people before God in our lives. The demons tremble at the sound of His name and this is why they fell down before Him. In this case, Jesus did not accept their worship, but sent them away. For Jesus knew that their day of judgment would soon come. Moreover, Jesus had and still has complete authority over Satan and his demonic kingdom. Are Mathew and Mark the only two to record the worshipping of Jesus?

Luke 24:52
And they worshiped Him...
John 9:38
Lord I believe and he worshiped Him...
Luke 24:51&52
Now it happened, while He (Jesus)*, blessed them, He was parted from them and carried up into heaven. And they worshiped Him and returned to Jerusalem with great joy.*

Jesus accepted worship and never rebuked anyone for his or her devotion toward Him, except for the false worship of fallen angels. Jesus never broke a commandment of God, He never broke the slightest letter of the law, and therefore, Jesus never sinned. If Jesus is not God, then His accepting God's worship would have made Him no better than Satan. Nevertheless, Jesus accepted the worship and never broke the command of God. Did the apostles or angels accept worship from men?

Acts 10:25&26
As Peter was coming in, Cornelius met him and fell down at his feet and worshiped him. But Peter lifted him up, saying, 'Stand up; I myself am also a man."

Peter corrected Cornelius as soon as he made the error of worshiping anything or anyone else besides God. Peter corrected him gently; nevertheless, he made it clear to Cornelius not to worship him.
We also read about the incident with Paul and Barnabas in the city of Lystra.
God had performed a mighty healing through the hand of Paul for a man who was born crippled in the presence of all, and when the people of the town saw this, they wanted to worship Paul and Barnabas.

Acts 14:11
Now when the people saw what Paul had done, they raised their voices, saying in the Lycaoninan language, "the gods have come down to us in the likeness of men"!

The text goes on to tell us that the people of the town were getting prepared to sacrifice animals to Paul and Barnabas as gods, which is a form of worship. We can see from the next verses that Paul and Barnabas stopped this as soon as they heard what the people were planning to do.

ACTS 14: 14 & 15
But when the Apostles Barnabas and Paul heard this, they tore their clothes and ran in among the multitude, crying out and saying, "Men, why are doing these things? We also are men with the same nature as you, and preached to you that you should turn from these useless things to the living God."

The apostles wasted no time in correcting these people by explaining to them that they were only men, and men or anything else are not to be worshiped, worship belongs to God. There was no hesitation on the part of Barnanas, Paul or Peter by not receiving worship, but confirmed the command that God alone should be our focus of worship, but Jesus accepted it.

We read in the book of Revelation how the Apostle John fell to the ground to worship an angel.

Revelation 22: 8&9
Now I, John, saw and heard these things. And when I heard and saw, I fell down to worship before the feet of the angel who showed me these things. Then he (the angel), *said to me, "See that you do not do that. For I am your fellow servant, and of your brethren the prophets, and of those who keep the words of this book. Worship God".*

The Angel wasted no time in correcting the apostle. God alone is to be worshiped! Although some people might want to be worshiped, and we know that Satan wants to be worshiped, God is clear on His instruction to us. He alone is God; He alone is to be worshiped.

We read further in the book of Revelation about the outcome of those who do worship Satan or his image.

Revelation 14: 9
If anyone worships the beast and his image, and receives his mark on his forehead or on his hand, he himself shall also drink of the wine of the wrath of God...

The book of Revelation tells us about three evil beings that come into view at the last days of the world. The beast, the false prophet and Satan are exposed and judged according to the promise of God. Satan sends the beast (the antichrist), and the false prophet to deceive humanity again. Notice how God warns us that even those who worshiped the beast's image will face the judgment of God. Does the beast's image represent a wood or stone image of the beast that all will be required to bow down before and worship? It is even more that that. I believe that the beast's image will also be all those evil things that the beast represents. The beast represents murder, lies, sexual immorality, deceitfulness, sorcerers, unforgiving and is against all that is holy. A person's image is all the things that he or she represents. Therefore, by willingly practicing what Satan represents, is nothing short of worshiping his image. In any event, worshiping anything or anybody besides God is a sin, a direct violation of the command of God and Jesus accepted worship! He rebuked many for their doubt, lack of faith and unbelief, but we never see Him refusing worship or correcting those who worshiped Him from a true heart

Psalm 45:11
Because He is your Lord, worship Him.

Hebrews 1: 8
"Let all the angels of God worship Him."

Draw a Hard Line

Isaiah 28:17
Also I will make justice the measuring line and
righteousness the plummet...

In an age of compromise, being politically correct and not invading anyone's rights, we see God laying it on the line, drawing a hard line of justice and righteousness. God is not attempting to impress any of us, nor will He compromise the truth for a lie. God tells us loud and clear that He will draw a line against those who oppose righteousness and forsake justice.

Some might say, 'what about the God of love we hear preached about every Sunday?' God is love, His very nature is love and He loves us with a divine, holy love. However, if any person or nation decides to live on the side of injustice and unrighteousness, then they have forsaken God's love and have made Satan their god since he is the ruler of unrighteousness and injustice. Therefore, those who practice such things are enemies of God, and God will draw a line as to how far He will allow evil to go. God will not excuse injustice, but He will expose it and judge it for what it is, unless those who practice injustice will repent and turn from their acts of evil.

Jesus drew a hard line when He entered the temple and saw people buying and selling their goods for profit instead of participating in prayer.

Matthew 21:12
Then Jesus went in to the temple of God and drove out all
those who bought and sold in the temple, and over turned
the tables of the moneychangers and the seats of those who
sold doves.

Jesus drew a hard line when He entered that temple and saw an operating flea market. Jesus was not concerned about His political image. The text says that Jesus flipped over tables, drove the merchants out and threw some chairs. Jesus did not compromise on justice, but expose the injustice for what it was.

Matthew 21:13
And He (Jesus), said, "It is written, My house shall be called a house of prayer, but you have made it a den of thieves."'

Jesus did not play any games when it came to dividing the truth from a lie, revealing injustice and proclaiming the righteousness of God, and drawing a hard line against evil. Therefore, are there lines that need to be drawn in our own lives? The first and most important line that needs to be drawn in the lives of every person that still has a heartbeat in their bodies is the line concerning who Jesus is. This is the beginning and the end of our eternal redemption and all hope for the present and for the future. Who is Jesus? As we explained in this book, the Scriptures reveal to us repeatedly His identity.

Philippians 2: 5, Hebrews 1: 3, Romans 1: 3 & 4, Galatians 1: 4, Galatians 2:20, 1ˢᵗ Peter 2:24, 1ˢᵗ Peter 3:22, Colossians 2:9
... Who, being in the form of God, did not consider it robbery to be equal with God.
...Who being in the brightness of His glory and the express image of His person...
...Who was born of the seed of David according to the flesh and declared the Son of God with power according to the Spirit of holiness...
...Who gave Himself for our sins, that He might deliver us from the present evil age...
...Who loved me and gave Himself for me...
... Who Himself bore our sins in His own body on a tree...
...Who has gone into heaven and is at the right hand of God, angels and authorities and powers having been made subject to Him.

For in Him (Jesus), dwells all the fullness of the Godhead in body form.

A line must be drawn between faith and unbelief, between justice and injustice. Moreover, on what side of the line do we stand? Do we believe Jesus to be who He says He is, who the apostles said He is, and who the prophets of old said He is? Are we going to believe Him or not? This is the eternal question that all of us must answer honestly and truthfully without doubt.
Jesus told us as plainly, and He did not leave us with a mystery in that we must spend a lifetime attempting to solve. Jesus told us the bottom line, the hard line that divides our eternities between heaven and hell.

John 13:6
Jesus said to him, "I am the way, the truth, and the life. No one comes to the Father except through Me."

Are we able to stand on both sides of the line, confessing to believe, yet acting as if we do not? Are we able to keep one foot in the worries of this world and the other foot in faith? Listen to what Jesus told the church of the Laodiceans in the book of Revelation.

Revelation 3: 15 & 16
"I know your works, that you are either cold or hot. I could wish you were cold or hot. So then, because you are lukewarm, and neither cold nor hot, I will vomit you out of My mouth."

Jesus makes it clear that being neutral is just as bad, if not worse than living in doubt. There is a line drawn between faith and doubt that must be divided and crossed. The apostles wrote about the false prophets, religions in error who attempt to strip the Lord Jesus of His deity, and make the claim that He was only a chosen vessel used by God as a messenger or an angelic being. This could not be farther from the truth. For the claims that Jesus made, the revelation that was given to the prophets and apostles all reveal His deity in the Godhead as God the Son.

Isaiah 9:6
And His name will be called Wonderful, Counselor, Mighty God, Everlasting Father, Prince of Peace.

For God bears witness through the prophets of old that Jesus left His position in the Godhead to become an eternal atonement for the sins of humanity, by the will of God the Father. God bears witness that He is called and is known as *Mighty God.* The Apostle John tells us clearly that there are three that bear witness to this truth. However, although they are three, they are one.

1st John 5:7
For there are three that bear witness in heaven: the Father, the Word (Jesus), *and the Holy Spirit: and these three are one.*

Jesus is the *Word* and the *Word is God.*

John 1:1 & 14
In the beginning was the Word (Jesus), *and the Word was with God, and the Word was God.*
And the Word (Jesus) *became flesh and dwelt among us.*

Two thousand years ago, God drew a line on a cross with the blood of mercy and grace. A line that has guaranteed the eternity for all those believe in the Son, and for those that doubt are reserved for eternal judgment. Jesus made it clear as to how to cross over the line.

John 13:6
"I am the way"

Do not bother to try another way, or a back door to heaven, there is none. Why is there no other way? Once we realize who Jesus is, then we can begin to understand what He has done and why He is the only way. To do this we need to think out of the box. What box am I talking about? The box of this present life, the few years here that is as one drop of water compared to the entire ocean of eternity. We may have 60, 70 or even 80 years here in this present life and then it is gone. Can we compare this to the endless time of eternity?

Jesus came to this world to teach us, to be our light from the darkness of doubt and unbelief. He came to give us a revelation of the Father's love for us and the understanding of His mercy. However, through everyday that He taught, healed and forgave the multitude that followed Him, He heard the cross calling. For it is only at the cross of Christ that we can truly realize why Jesus is the only way for mankind to be redeemed from the judgment of sin. It is at the cross that we can know without a doubt our eternal destiny. At the cross, we can know the love that God the Father has for us, because it is the only way that God has provided for us. For this sacrifice needed to be given only once. However, there is a dividing line that must be drawn and crossed; it is the line between faith and doubt. We come to God by faith, and not by works, thinking that our self-righteousness will grant us a place in the kingdom of God. It is not our righteousness that was offered as an eternal sacrifice for sin, but the blood of Jesus Christ, His righteousness has washed away the ugly stain of sin. We need to draw a hard line in our minds that will lead our souls in faith.

Philippians 2: 5
Let this mind be in you which was also in Christ Jesus.

For it is in our minds that the enemy has waged war for the possession and destruction of our spirits. His weapons are doubt and unbelief by the power of suggestion. His bait is the temporary pleasures and riches of this life in an attempt to blind us from the true treasure of knowing and loving God for eternity. He will play on any insecurity that holds us captive. He will attempt to distort and pervert the true purpose of our lives. The line must be drawn as to whether we are going to believe and trust God by the power of His word, or we are going to trust the lies of the enemy. The choice is ours, we can choose to live in the presence of God in His victory, or be a victim in the defeat of darkness, doubt and unbelief. We must choose and draw a hard line between faith and doubt and step over the line to faith. The line is the question: Who is Jesus?

Hebrews 1:8
But to the Son (Jesus), *He,* (the Father) *says:*
Your throne, O God, is forever and ever.

Who is He?

He is the *Son of God, our Savoir, our Rock,* the great *I AM,*
our *Redeemer, the Author and Finisher of our faith,* our
Mediator, the True Vine, Wonderful Counselor and *Mighty
God.* He alone is our eternal hope as the final blood sacrifice
for all our sins. He holds our eternal destiny, and unto Him,
all of the angels in heaven surrender their worship. To Him
every knee shall bow and every tongue will confess before
the throne of grace. He is our peace: *the Prince of Peace*
and our rest and strength through the storm. He is the *Great
Shepherd, the Resurrection.* He is *the Way, the Truth, and
the Life.* He is our *Creator, our Healer,* and the *true Judge.*
He holds the keys to paradise; He is the living *Word,* the
manifestation of God. He is the *Beginning and the End,* the
Alpha and the Omega. He is the *Lamb* who was slaughtered
for the sake of the fold. He is our joy in the knowledge of our
redemption by the power of His love through His mercy. He
is our *Comforter* who can associate with our earthly burdens
and understands our trials and tribulations. He is our *Brother*
in the sense that He also lived in the same vessel that we
now live in. He was tempted, as we are tempted, yet without
sin. He is the *Holy One,* unblemished and without mark or
wrinkle. He is the *Anointed One of God.* He is *Love* in the
purest form. He is the *Light, the true Light* who lights the
hearts of men and women coming into the world. In Him,
there is no darkness. He is our *righteousness* and our
freedom, for through Him we have been set free from the
bondage of the law of sin and death. He is our eternal *Gift*
and the true testimony of God. He is the *potter* who molds
us into vessels of honor, and of love. He is our *example,* the
perfect letter for us to copy. He is the *Promise* foretold by
the prophets of old, as they saw the forgiving, redeeming
power of God. He is *Faithful* to do all that had been written
concerning the life we now live and life eternal. He has a
*name above every name in heaven, or on the earth or under
the earth. His kingdom shall see no end*; He is over every
kingdom, every dominion, and every principality. He is the

King of all kings, in total supremacy of all! Yet, He is gentle, kind, faithful, trustworthy, merciful, forgiving, loving, dependable, truthful, and knows the heart of every man, woman and child. He is the *Giver and Sustainer of all life*. He is the *Chief Corner Stone* in which we are built as a temple where the Spirit of God lives. He is the *Head of the church,* as we are His body, and in Him, we live. He is the *true bread* who fills the hearts and minds of all those who believe in Him. He is the *Apostle* sent from God. He is our *High Priest* who makes intercession for us in the presence of the Almighty Father God. He was born into this world and put to death in the natural, but was resurrected in glory by the supernatural power of God. He is the *Lion of the tribe of Judah, the Root of David* and the *King of the Jews*. He is the *Lamb of God*. He is all these and more; nevertheless, He is a *Man*.

The Apostle Thomas looked at this Man, who was standing and talking in front of him with fatal wounds, yet this Man is alive! Thomas's response was one that brings us to the realization of His deity.

John 20:28
And Thomas answered Him, "My Lord and my God."

If you have never believed Jesus Christ before, or believed Him at one time and your light of faith has now become dim, you have an opportunity to change it. Moreover, if you have been a victim of false teaching, that can be nothing more then empty rituals of religion and will not fill the emptiness inside of you, you can change it. Now no one can change without repentance. Repentance is a cry to God to change, to turn from sin and to turn to God in faith. Faith is the key ingredient and the outward confession of repentance in faith to God from the heart will send your words before the throne of mercy by the authority of His name, Jesus Christ. For it is the prayer in faith, and not by our own so-called righteousness, that brings us to the place of salvation. After all, what could we add to the cross of Christ? He was the

Perfect Sacrifice. Moreover, it is the *gift of God*. We cannot work for a gift since a gift is freely given. If we needed to work for our eternal redemption, then it would not be a *gift* from God, but a wage as payment due.

Romans 10: 9
That if you confess with your mouth the Lord Jesus Christ and believe in your heart that God raised from Him the dead, you will be saved.

However, we also need to come to God with a humble heart, a heart of repentance, and a heart that is willing to change, to be molded by the Potter's hands. Ask God in your own words to forgive every sin, and tell Him that you are truly sorrowful for every wrong you might have done. Confess to Him that you believe that Jesus Christ died on the cross in your place, taking the punishment for sin that rightly belongs to you and me. This prayer in faith will cause God to wipe the slate clean. You will be His child and your name will be recorded in heaven, in the *Book of Life* as God's very own for now and eternity. The very Spirit of God will live inside of you. Could anything in all of heaven and earth be worth more than that? Eternal life in the very presence of God is by far the most valuable gift that anyone could possibly receive. This gift can be refused, but if you believe, God will hear your confession of faith with a heart of repentance, and you will be saved...
Jesus said, *"Repent and believe in the gospel."*
"...And lo, I am with you always, even to the end of the age."
The simple formula is to repent, turn from sin, and believe in the redeeming quality of God's love, Jesus Christ. And Jesus promises that He is then with us forever, a time with no end.

Scripture taken from:
King James Version

New King James Version
New American Standard
The New Testament in the Language of the People
C. Williams
The New Testament in the Language of Today
W. Beck

2nd Peter 1: 20, 21
Knowing this first, that no prophecy or Scripture is of any
private interpretation, for prophecy never came by man, but
holy men of God spoke as they were moved by the Holy
Spirit.